on tuesday the boxer played dead

ANN RUSSELL

APOCRYPHILE
PRESS

Apocryphile Press
PO Box 255
Hannacroix, NY 12087
www.apocryphilepress.com

Please join our mailing list at www.apocryphilepress.com/free. We'll keep you
up-to- date on all our new releases, and we'll also send you a FREE BOOK. Visit
us today!

contents

one

"I've never seen so many dogs in one place in my life," Jack said, his mouth open in wonder.

"Welcome to the wonderful world of dog shows," I said, bumping his shoulder with my own. The Gold County Fairground was literally overrun with canine prima donnas and their anxious humans. I held Scout's leash next to my leg, keeping the brindle Boxer as close as possible lest her tender paws be trampled by the crowd. I noted with some approval that Jack was keeping his three-legged mutt Tripod on a short leash as well. If their buzzing tails were any indication, both dogs were having a grand time. And the day had just begun.

"Wow," Jack said, shaking his head. I tried to remember my first dog show, but it was lost in the fog of memory. I had always enjoyed the excitement, the crush of people and dogs, the suspense—especially when a dog I owned or knew was competing.

I didn't know any of the competing dogs today, but that hardly mattered. It was a treat just to be there. "First up, Boxer Conformation," I said.

"Hold up," Jack said, "Confirmation? Is a bishop going to slap the dogs' cheeks?"

I looked at him as if his forehead had sprouted a unihorn. "What in the world are you talking about?"

"Confirmation is a sacrament," Jack explained, shrugging. "What else can it mean?"

I sometimes had to remind myself that Jack, an Episcopal priest, lived in a slightly different universe than I did. "No, you hopeless church geek. Not con-FUR-mation, it's con-FOR-mation. Conformation is the dog-show word for 'beauty pageant.'"

"Oh. You learn something every day," Jack said.

I pulled the program from my back pocket and scanned it. "It starts in fifteen minutes, just enough time to hit the restroom and grab a soda. That way." I pointed out a path through the hubbub.

"Here we go, then," Jack said.

Fourteen minutes later, we helped Tripod and Scout navigate to a seat on a low riser, with a terrific view of the ring. Actually, there were a dozen rings spread out over the fairgrounds. But this was the one the Boxers showed at. I consulted the program again as the handlers led their dogs into the ring, sprinting around its circumference.

"Are those the owners?" Jack asked.

"They can be, but usually they aren't," I answered. "Having a beautiful dog is only half the battle. The other half is knowing how to handle it. Most owners hire professional handlers for their turn in the ring."

"Huh. That's a novel job description," Jack mused aloud. "Is that, like, their full-time job?"

"Most of them, yeah," I answered.

"Well, I'll be..."

"That one there—see the smallish fawn? She comes from a

breeder I know who named her business Salad Days. So the dog's full name is Salad Days Top Gun, but she goes by Filly."

"Isn't Filly a young horse?" Jack asked.

"Yes, and apparently a small Boxer."

"Does the dog show world start to make sense eventually, or does it just stay weird?" Jack asked.

"It pretty much stays weird," I answered. "But you adjust." I waited a beat, then added, "Not unlike church."

"Touché," he said with a chuckle.

The judge took six dogs through their paces and awarded a winner. It wasn't Filly, but that didn't surprise me. Filly was a fine-looking dog, but not a stunner. That honor went to a brindle bitch with shoulders like a linebacker. I felt a prick in my heart that said, *I want to be the mother of champions.* It was a haughty, aggressive, persistent voice. Jack would probably call it a temptation, but I kept quiet about it. Instead, I innocently turned to Scout and said, "How would you like a packmate, Scout?"

Jack's eyebrows rose, but he said nothing.

I felt heat rise to my cheeks. "I've always wanted to see a bitch through her championship."

"Scout isn't champion material?" Jack asked.

I gave him a piteous look. He was so innocent. "First, she's spayed, which disqualifies her for conformation. Second, she doesn't have the posture."

"Sounds like a temptation," Jack said.

I made a face.

"What? What did I say?" Jack asked.

"Nothing, it's just that...I think I already know you too well."

"Is that a bad thing?" he asked. He looked truly confused.

Instead of answering, I put my free arm through his and led

him further into the fairgrounds. "Rally starts in half an hour," I said.

"What's Rally?" Jack asked.

"It's like an obstacle course," I said. "I think you'll get a kick out of it. And any dog can compete, even mutts. If you like it, you should try it out with Tripod. He'd love it."

"Can't wait," Jack said. "Oh, wait. You're trying to get me involved in your dog cult. That was sneaky."

"You do your proselytizing, I do mine," I said.

"You are landing every punch today," he joked.

"How is that different from any other day?" I asked. But before he could think of a comeback, I said, "What do you want to do before Rally? Basically, we have two choices: We can go shopping—the merch room is in that building there." I pointed it out.

"Merch?" he asked.

"Imagine a football-field-sized pet store," I said.

"The mind reels," he said.

"There's a lot of redundancy," I explained. "But some one-of-a-kind things you will see nowhere else, too."

"Dog crafts?" His eyebrows rose.

"Dog crafts," I affirmed.

"What's the other choice?" he asked.

"We could take a walk through the grooming area—it's where everyone hangs out between their times in the ring. Every dog and their owner have to basically camp out some-where when they're not showing. So there are a lot of very pretty dogs to look at, all sorted by breed."

"No mutts, though?" he asked.

"No mutts. Sorry."

"Can you tell me what breeds we're looking at?" he asked.

"Absolutely. And if I don't recognize something, we can ask."

"Okay. Let's go see some dogs," he said cheerfully.

I led him to the grooming area. I could tell he was impressed. The grooming tents stretched on for what seemed like forever, and they were packed with dogs of all breeds and sizes. The air was cacophonous with yelps, barks, whines, and howls. There was a lot of human chatter, too, laughter and swearing and gossip. It was glorious—at least I thought so.

"It's a little overwhelming," Jack said.

"Just let it wash over you," I said. "Here are the Border Collies." I pointed to a section with about twenty or so heterochromous dogs, some of them in their crates, some on leashes carefully clutched by their owners, and some up on grooming tables, preparing for their moment in the ring.

"What are Border Collies like?" Jack asked.

"Think of them as the dogs that have both a PhD and Attention Deficit Hyperactivity Disorder. They're whip smart, but you have to give them a job to do or they'll drive you crazy."

"Sounds like a handful," Jack said.

"Those are the Jack Russell terriers," I said, pointing to a section housing much smaller dogs.

Just then a voice rose above the hubbub. "Doctor! Oh, Doctor Gibbons!"

I whirled around, looking for the owner of the voice, and found it in Teri Mankowitz, scurrying toward me. She had a pile of red hair on top of her head and orange plastic earrings that begged to be returned to the 1960s.

"Friend of yours?" Jack asked.

"Client," I said. "She has a Jack Russell named Sputnik."

Teri stopped just short of plowing into me, looking flustered, as if she didn't know whether to extend her hand or give me a hug. This is California, so she settled on the hug. I politely returned it. "Hey, Teri. Is Sputnik competing?"

"He is!" She pointed over her shoulder. "George is getting him ready."

"Well, best of luck," I said.

"Is this your dog?" She knelt by Scout, who began to sniff at her pile of hair.

"Yes, this is Scout." I turned to Jack. "This is my friend Jack and his dog Tripod."

She glanced at Tripod, noticed that he was only a three-legged mutt, and promptly ignored both owner and dog.

"What does Scout do?" she asked.

It was tempting to be offended by the question. She might be innocently asking if I was showing her, but it sounded suspiciously like "What is she good for?" I decided to be politic. "Well, we've been working on a new trick. Want to see?"

She stood fully upright again, her painted-on eyebrows high on her forehead, clearly not expecting my response. Before she could answer, I said, "Scout, sit." Scout sat. "Scout, down." Scout lay down. "Scout, play dead." Whereupon Scout turned over on her side and lay still. The only problem was that she kept one eye open, my face never out of sight.

"Close your eye," I said, slightly irritated. Her tail started to wag, thumping happily on the ground. I sighed. "Clearly we have some work to do."

Teri patted my arm as if consoling me for a death in the family. "There, there. There's a trick title this year. Why don't you enter her next year? It'll give you something to work toward. She doesn't have to be perfect!"

I wondered if I was perfect enough not to punch her. But I realized that would be bad for business. Jack's face wore an innocently bemused smile.

"Well, got to go. We're up in fifteen. Toodles!"

"Uh...toodles," I said, waving weakly as she trundled off through the crowd.

"Toodles," Jack said.

"Shut up," I said blackly.

"Is everybody that eccentric here?" Jack asked.

"She's a mild case," I answered.

"Huh. Also like church," he said.

In spite of myself, I smiled. Just then a scream erupted, cutting through the hubbub like a lighthouse beacon through fog.

"What the hell?" Jack asked.

"Vet! Vet! I need a vet!" a voice shouted, followed by another scream.

I yanked on the leash and pulled Scout in close as I jogged toward the source of the screaming. Fortunately, the piercing noise had made everyone stop—navigating quickly around stationary bodies was much easier than around bodies in motion. In a few seconds, I beheld the screamer. Scout rushed ahead of me, straining on her lead as we got close. I quickly took in the scene. A German Shepherd was splayed out on the ground, its legs twitching in the direction of the ceiling. Foam spilled from its muzzle, and its eyes were glassy and distant.

I lunged for the dog, shouting, "I'm a vet. Whose dog is this?" Scout was sniffing around the dog. I checked his pupils—they were tiny. I checked his pulse. Racing. And then it wasn't. The dog jerked, bashing its head on the cement floor. Then it lay still.

"Anselm!" a woman screamed. I looked up.

"Is this your dog?"

"Yes," she said, not taking her eyes off the beast. She wrung her hands as her lip quivered.

"Do I have your permission to take some drastic measures?"

"Yes!"

I punched the dog in the chest, then began compressions. I

tried to seal its muzzle, ignoring the foam, and breathed into it. I kept this up for several minutes, but the dog was still as a stone. Scout whined as I worked. Finally, I sat back on my haunches and looked up at the owner again. "I'm sorry. He's gone."

"No...no...my Anselm!" She launched herself at his body; I scooted back to give her room. She pressed herself on top of him and sobbed. Jack offered me his hand and I took it, standing up. I put my hand on her shoulder and gave it a squeeze. "I'm so sorry."

She was oblivious, however. Her shoulders shook and she began to wail.

"Give her some space, please," Jack said, and the volume he was able to achieve while still sounding compassionate surprised me. But then it occurred to me that he'd had a lot of practice at it. The press of people around the woman and her dog backed up a halting step or two. "Further, please," Jack bellowed. The crowd responded with an awkward shuffle backward.

"What's going on here?" a man's voice cut through the silence of the hall. He pushed his way through the throng until he broke into the empty circle. Then he stopped, his eyes growing wide and his jaw instantly going slack. "Holy—" He looked at the woman. "Betty, is he okay?"

She didn't answer, but her wailing renewed at a higher pitch. She rocked back and forth over the dog, still covering most of it with her body. "What happened?"

I handed Scout's leash to Jack, stepped over Betty's legs, and approached the man. He was very tall—I came up to about his sternum. He also had as square a jaw as I have ever seen. I held out my hand. "I'm Doctor Casey Gibbons. I'm sorry, this dog is dead. Who are you?"

He blinked, still looking at the dog. Eventually he tore his

gaze away and looked at my face, then back at the dog. "I'm...
I'm his handler."

I pulled out my phone and began taking notes. I entered
the time of death, typing as fast as I could with my thumbs.
"This dog is named Anselm?" I asked.

"Uh...yes," the handler said, still not looking at me.

"Full name?" I asked.

"Uh...Deputy Dogs High Flyer."

I noted that. "Age?"

"Three...I think."

"Your name?" I asked.

"Austin Teal."

"Contact info? Phone number first."

It was like pulling teeth, but eventually I got what I needed
out of the distracted handler, including the name and contact
info of the owner.

"Any idea what he might have gotten ahold of?" I asked.

"Y...You mean, like, poison?" He actually looked at me. His
hair was dark and wavy, and I noticed again how photogenic
his square jaw was.

"You tell me," I said.

"What's this?" Another voice cut through the crowd. A
moment later, an older man in a lab coat pushed through.
"What happened?" he asked.

This must be the show vet. I stepped back over Betty's legs
and approached the man. I introduced myself and gave him a
quick recap. "Are you willing to file?" he asked.

"Sure," I said, holding up my phone. "I've got all the info."

He nodded. I looked at his name tag—Dr. Tony Pressman. I
added that to my notes. I asked Dr. Pressman if he wanted to
examine the dog, but he didn't want to disturb Betty in her
grief. And it didn't matter at this point; he could wait. The dog
wasn't going to get any worse...or any better. Pressman and I

exchanged contact information and I put my hand on Betty's shoulder one last time before taking Scout's leash back from Jack. The crowd parted for us without too much trouble, and I shuddered at just how claustrophobic I was feeling.

"I need to get to an open space," I said.

"Of course," Jack said. "This way."

I found my breathing was easier the more distance we put between ourselves and the crowd. Then Jack turned and looked at the whole scene. I joined him and felt his arm around me, pulling me toward himself. I leaned into him, grateful for the comfort. It wasn't my dog, but that didn't mean it wasn't traumatic. My heart went out to Betty. The handler had told me her last name was Swann. *Poor Betty Swann,* I thought. I tried to imagine how I would feel if something like that had happened to Scout. I immediately banished the thought—it was too terrible.

"Have you ever seen anything like this before?" Jack asked.

"At a dog show? No," I answered. "But at work, this is a Tuesday."

two

I was still rattled the next day. I showed up for work a little early, but it did little good; I was finding it hard to focus. I had to read my first client's chart three times before comprehension kicked in.

My second client had cancelled, so I had a welcome break in the midst of what was shaping up to be an otherwise busy morning. I rounded the corner to the reception desk and was surprised to see no one behind it.

"Where is Stacy?" I asked no one. But then I saw. She was holding the door open for the UPS man. There was good reason for that. He was maneuvering a hand truck stacked with boxes so high I was afraid the slightest bump would send the whole thing crashing onto his head. But, as so often with waiters juggling multiple plates, my fears did not materialize this time either. He parked the stack near the reception desk and asked Stacy for a signature.

Stacy was a rotund, no-nonsense mother of four who had recently started with us. She had come in the very first day, sweetly learned the lay of the land, and immediately started barking orders. Drill sergeants had nothing on Stacy. Ellie had complained, but I'd encouraged her to give the new receptionist a chance. It had paid off. Within a week, everything was running much more smoothly, and her fierce demeanor had served to diminish conflict, not generate it.

I, for one, was grateful for someone else to play the heavy for once. This Stacy did without complaint, and seemingly without thought. I started thinking of her as The Organizer and wondered if we even needed an office manager with her on board.

"What is all that?" I asked once the UPS man was gone.

Stacy brought the cat's-eye glasses hanging around her neck by a lanyard up to her face and, without actually putting them on, peered through the lenses at the packing slip.

"Ay-er-veedic herbs?" she frowned. "Dr. Singh!"

Dr. Ajeet Singh speed-walked out of the break room, wiping his mouth with a paper napkin. "Yes, Miss Stacy?" He noticed me and smiled. "Good morning, Casey."

"Morning, Ajeet," I said.

"Can you take a look at these, please?" Stacy pointed to the boxes. They towered over her, threatening to topple at the faintest gust of air.

"Certainly." He strode to where she was standing. He wasn't much taller than she was, but his shoulders were broad, and his quick energy reminded me of a cocker spaniel. The gold lamé turban he had worn in his application photo had been replaced by a workaday light blue turban that contrasted pleasingly with his navy scrubs. A tiny ceremonial dagger was fixed to his belt.

"What is this?" He stooped a bit to look at the packing slip.

"That's what I want to know," Stacy said. "What is that in your beard? Is that a chickpea?"

"Oh, dear." He fumbled at his beard, found the offending

chickpea and popped it into his mouth. "I was saving it for later," he joked, his face flushing.

Stacy looked at me and rolled her eyes.

I chuckled silently and folded my arms, leaning against the wall behind the desk. I had no other place to be, after all, and watching the culture clash between Ajeet and Stacy was nothing if not entertaining.

"Oh! These are my herbs!" His face lit up.

"What herbs? We don't stock herbs," Stacy said.

"But...well, we do now!" Ajeet waggled his head. I knew that was an Indian thing, but I didn't know what it meant. I doubted Stacy did either. Ajeet was all-American. His accent was Southern California all the way. He had told me about playing baseball as a kid. But he had also told me about the Indian traditions his parents kept alive. Apparently the head-waggle had made the transition from one generation to the next.

"What do they do?" she asked.

"They restore *dosha* to the *doshas*—"

"In English, please."

"In Ayurvedic medicine, illness results when the three elemental humors are out of balance. Using the herbs, we bring them back into harmony, restoring health to our patients and... making everyone happy." He gave her a weak smile. I could tell he was trying to maintain his chipper demeanor, but Stacy wasn't making it easy.

Stacy looked at me. "Did you approve this?"

"I don't need to approve it," I said. "The man is a veterinarian."

"Do you even have training in this kind of...*medicine*?" She said the last word with obvious distaste, as if she had found a bug in her soup.

"I have a certificate in Ayurvedic Veterinary Care from the Ojai Dharma Institute," Ajeet affirmed.

"B-but who's going to *want* this kind of treatment?" Stacy almost wailed.

"We're in the gold country of California," I said. "*Lots* of people."

"I suppose you're going to start sticking cats with needles next?" Stacy narrowed her eyes at Ajeet.

"Oh, yes! I have my acupuncture kit ready to go. Please do let our clients know."

Stacy pointed her finger at me. "We need to talk."

I smiled at her noncommittally. She walked off in a huff. Ajeet sidled up to me. "I don't think she likes me."

"She adores you," I said.

"She has a very strange way of showing her affection, then."

"How are you doing?" I asked him. We were usually too busy to make small talk, but I had been wondering how my new hire was adjusting.

"Oh, just fine, I think. Perhaps not if you ask Miss Stacy. But...you have not heard any complaints, have you?"

"Me? No. People like you."

"I've been thinking of trying something," he said, looking a little sheepish.

"Is this about the herbs?"

"What? No, no! It's something else."

"I can't wait," I said. But before he could tell me his idea, we were interrupted by Ellie, waving at me from her computer. She pointed toward the door. "Lawyer approaching on your six."

"On my what?"

"Behind you," Ajeet said. "A woman in a business suit just came through the door."

I turned and beheld our attorney, Fuchsia Carhart, with her natty attire, slender legs, and blond bob. I let slip an "Ugh..." but was immediately sorry.

"I heard that," Fuchsia said. She stopped just on the other side of the reception desk.

"Sorry."

She shrugged. "I'm used to it. A lawyer is never good news." She flipped her hair to one side with a jerk of her head. "Can we talk?"

"Joy," I said, a little too loudly. "Sure."

Ellie called out, "Three is open."

Ajeet and I were the only vets there, so I knew they were all open. But Three was as good as any other. I waved Ms. Carhart toward Exam Room Three's outer door, while I turned and took the back way to its inner door. When I entered, she was already seated, legs crossed, a professional smile on her face.

"It's always a pleasure, Ms. Carhart," I said.

"In the same way that a lanced boil is pleasurable, I'm sure," she said.

I almost snorted, and we both laughed. I caught a glimpse of a real person in her eyes for a moment, and I felt something shift inside me. "I'm sorry," I said. "It's just..."

"I know exactly how it is. It's not any fun for me, either."

"So why do you do it?"

"I don't suppose you enjoy putting animals down, or relating a bad diagnosis..."

"No," I admitted. "I hate that part of the job."

She just nodded. "We all have 'parts' we hate."

"I suppose we do. Well, best to rip the band-aid off all at once. To what do I owe the pleasure of your visit?"

"We've had a development."

In the lawsuit, she meant. A few months ago, a scam artist named Margaret "Maggie" Edgerton had poisoned her dog specifically so that he would die on the operating table, intending to sue the vet. Maggie's problem was that her vet—and my best friend, Shelley—had been murdered. My problem was that Maggie was now suing the practice instead.

"Uh...a good development or a bad development?" I asked.

"I received this in discovery," she passed a file folder to me. I opened it with considerable trepidation. It had to be bad news, after all. What I found was a file on me, containing information on my employment for the past ten years or so.

"Okay..."

"You didn't tell me you'd been fired," Fuchsia said.

"You didn't ask, and it's nobody's business," I said, feeling a cold finger tickling at my spine.

"It is now," she said. "I want the details, because this is going to come out."

I sighed. I had moved to Gold County specifically to get a fresh start—not just after my divorce, but professionally as well. "Let's call it a personality conflict," I suggested.

"Let's go into a bit more detail," she countered.

"In San Diego, I worked for a clinic that was part of a chain —you know, one of those corporate monstrosities that gobbles up private practices and then controls what the vets can and can't do, all in the interest of greater profit for the shareholders."

Fuchsia was writing on a yellow legal pad while I spoke. "That was VET, Inc., yes?"

"That's right. You couldn't pass wind in that practice without clearing it with corporate. One night we got an emergency case just before closing—dog got hit by an SUV. A passerby brought him in—no tags. I knew I could save the dog by amputating the back leg. Corporate told me to put him to sleep."

"So...you gave corporate the finger and saved the dog."

"Of course I did," I said.

She wrote furiously. I waited until she was done. "Is that it?" she asked, looking up.

"That's it. So I was canned for insubordination, or not following orders, or whatever."

Fuchsia rummaged through her notes. "Failure to comply with corporate guidelines."

"Sure. That'll do."

"Nothing more sinister there?"

"Nope."

"Any other skeletons lurking in your closet?"

"Like...?"

"You tell me."

I shook my head. "Not that I can think of. But just because my conscience is clear doesn't mean other people don't think crazy things."

"Always true. Do you happen to know about any of these 'crazy things'?"

"Nothing comes to mind," I said.

"Fair enough. Can anyone corroborate your side of the story?"

"I imagine corporate records will tell the same story," I said.

"We'll see." She stood. "Thank you for your time, doctor."

"Sure," I said.

"Buck up," Fuchsia said, reaching out and touching my sleeve. "The trial will be here before you know it, and then it will all be over."

"And I'll either be fine or I'll have to close down Shelley's practice."

"It's your practice now."

"It'll always be Shelley's practice," I said.

She nodded and reached for the door. But before she

opened it, she turned back. "Hey, you wanna catch a drink sometime?"

I blinked. "Uh...as in a 'let's-bitch-about-our-jobs' drink, or a 'let's-go-on-a-date' drink?"

"We're just getting to know each other, so let's say the former."

I momentarily lost the power of speech. It was so incredibly kind, and ever since Shelley had died, I realized that I had no girlfriends. I cleared my throat. "I would love that."

"There's a wine bar in Utah City, Dalliance—do you know it?"

"I've seen it," I said.

"I'll text you. We can meet up and..." she shrugged, "...bitch about our jobs."

"That sounds...lovely," I said.

She smiled and let herself out.

I stood alone for a moment in the empty examination room. It felt like an important moment. I had not considered Fuchsia friend material. That she saw me that way surprised and delighted me. Jack might say it felt like a moment of grace.

three

I was tired after work, but seeing Scout's excitement about getting in the car made me rethink my own feelings. She didn't know where she was going, but she was raring to go. I didn't blame her—after all, she'd been cooped up alone in the cottage all day. I, on the other hand, was ready for a hot bath and a whiskey. I reminded myself that going to Jack's for dinner could be relaxing too, and whiskey was definitely part of that picture. I wondered if the bath was also still possible, but warned myself against being silly...or too forward.

I still didn't know what to think of Jack. He was cute as a button. He was also whip smart and funny. He had a laid-back sensibility that I envied. But he was also religious, and that... troubled me. He wasn't *crazy* religious, I was relieved to admit, but any amount of religious was a red flag. And he was a *priest*. He had dived into the deep end, there was no getting around it. Could I live with that? A voice I recognized as my Wiser Self asked a better question: Could I come to appreciate it? I didn't know the answer to that.

As soon as I turned onto Jack's street, the stub of Scout's

tail began to clock back and forth, and if it was possible for a dog her size to pace in the passenger seat, she did that too. Whatever misgivings I might be having, it was clear that Scout loved Jack, with her whole Boxer heart—and in general she was a good judge of character.

I parked on the street outside the church. I knew I could probably park in the lot, but it felt like trespassing or intruding or something. It was a concession I wasn't yet willing to make, although what it was conceding to I had no rational idea. Not bothering to put a leash on Scout, we walked around the church building to the dense copse of trees behind the sanctuary. I had come to think of it as the Black Forest, as it shrouded the spooky mock-tudor parsonage in perpetual gloom.

I knocked on the door, and within seconds it swung open to reveal Jack's bright grin. "Hey! It's my two favorite girls!" he said with undeniable gusto. Tripod leaped in the air as well as a three-legged dog can, and the two dogs instantly began to sniff their greetings.

Seeing Jack's face, I felt the tiredness melt out of my bones. *Who needs a bath when I've got him*, a voice in my head said, and he caught me up in a bear hug. I returned it in my more subdued fashion, and then Jack dropped to all fours and began nuzzling foreheads with Scout. Tripod was not having this, however, and inserted his head between Jack and Scout's. Jack hugged both dogs, then rolled over and asked, "How was work?"

Are there three words any better than these in the English language, when spoken with sincerity? I didn't think so. "It was just fine. We had a light morning, and...I don't know, but I might have made a friend."

"Really?" He stood up. "That sounds promising."

"I hope so. We'll see. It's Fuchsia Carhart, our lawyer. She asked me out for a glass of wine."

"Lovely. I hope you're going to go." He followed Scout and Tripod over to the couch by the fire. It was blazing away cheerfully. He sat and patted the seat next to him. Scout leaped up, turned once and obliged him. Tripod, however, sat on his dog bed before the fire, his eyes never leaving his master. Jack stroked Scout's forehead and said, "Uh, Scout, honey, I was hoping your mom would sit there." Scout just put her head on her paws and stared at the fire. "Huh. Sorry."

"It's okay. There's room on the other side of her." With the dog between us, I sat with a sigh. Jack reached for the carafe of whisky on the coffee table and poured two fingers in each of the glasses. He handed one to me. "To a lovely evening with just the five of us."

"You and me, Scout and Tripod, and..."

"Well, Jesus of course. He's everywhere."

"Of course." I shook my head as I took a sip. That was exactly the kind of thing that worried me about Jack.

"Anyway, I do hope you go."

"I will. I've...I realized that since Shelley died, I don't really have any friends."

"You have me. And Sarge—"

"I mean girlfriends," I said. "Women need other women, just as men need other men."

"That's true," Jack said. "That's exactly why you should go."

I did not disagree with that. "Who do you hang out with?" I asked. "Who are your guy friends?"

"Well, that's a problem," he said. He took a sip. "I was called to St. Julian's-in-the-Valley two years ago—"

"Where were you before?" I asked.

"Stockton."

"Ugh," I said. "So, a promotion."

"In every sense," he said. "But I left some good friends

there. A pastors' bowling league. The Methodist minister, Budd Collins. We'd become pretty good friends."

"What did you do together?"

He slunk into his chair. "We...uh...used to get together once a week to drink whiskey and watch Battlestar Galactica."

I blinked. "Really?"

"Really. In uniform."

"You mean in your clergy outfits?"

"No, I mean in Battlestar Galactica regalia. I could show you...sometime..." He slunk even further down into his seat.

I laughed. This weird bit of information delighted me for some reason. "And here?"

"Well, the only people I know here are church people, and I'm not really allowed to be friends with my parishioners."

"Really? Isn't that...hard to do?"

"It can be, especially in a small town like this." He shrugged. "I've reached out to the other pastors, and have even had lunch with a few, but I haven't really clicked with anyone."

"It's hard to find someone to dress up as a spaceman with." I shook my head, mock-commiserating.

"You're making fun of me," he said.

"A little bit," I admitted. I leaned over the dog and planted a kiss on his cheek. "But it's good-natured."

He swallowed, and there was an odd look in his eye. A frightened look. A hungry look. He set his tumbler down on the coffee table, then leaned over the dog himself. His face came closer to mine, and I met his eyes. He was very close, but he held back, waiting to see if I would move forward to meet him. I did, and for a brief, electric moment, my lips brushed his.

He pulled back and smiled at me. "That was...nice."

I nodded my agreement. "It was."

"Can I kiss you again?" he asked.

"I'd like that," I said.

He leaned in again, and this time when I met those amazing angular lips of his, I didn't let go. I pressed into him and felt drunk on much more than the small amount of whiskey I'd had. I felt the flick of his tongue on my lips and I opened to it, wanting more of him.

Apparently, we were making things uncomfortable for Scout. She excused herself and found a new place on the floor by the fire, leaving an empty space between Jack and myself. I scooted into it, and pressed myself hard against his chest, seeking his mouth with mine again. A delirious current ran between us and I sucked hungrily on his tongue as I caressed the stubble on his cheeks with my hands.

After a timeless, blissful interval, I pulled back and licked the wet from my lips. He reached for my hand and held it tight.

"I have a question for you," he said.

"Okay." I was grateful for the conversation, as I really needed to catch my breath.

"I need to take some vacation days. And I was thinking of heading over to Yosemite soon. And I wanted to know if...well, if maybe you'd like to come with me."

"You mean...go on vacation together?"

"Well, it's not far, and it's just a weekend, but...yeah. What do you think?"

I swallowed. I didn't know what to think. I felt my pulse race and I felt even more lightheaded. As attractive as Jack was, as much as I liked him, his religiosity still scared me.

"Would we be...sharing a room?"

"If you like. Or if you're not ready, we could get two rooms." He shrugged. "Whatever you're most comfortable with."

"I..." I looked away. My eyes landed on my sleeping dog. I looked back at him. I smiled. "I'm...I'm just not ready for that. I'm sorry."

"It's okay. It really is. I'm sorry if I was...moving too fast."

"It is kind of fast. I mean...we've only just now had our first kiss."

"That's true." He looked a little sad, but he tried to hide it.

"How about a second kiss?" I asked.

"What, now?" he asked.

"Now," I said, leaning into him again.

four

The next day at the clinic was busy, and I didn't give a flying fig. I was standing at the copier, making duplicates of some notes for an insurance claim, when suddenly Ellie was by my side.

"Okay, what's going on?" she asked.

"What do you mean?" I returned innocently.

"I mean that you've been utterly checked out, standing in front of a copier—which is *not* running, may I point out—with a stupid grin on your face. And don't get me started on your dreamy lizard eyes."

"I have lizard eyes?" I asked.

She narrowed one eye at me. "And now you're blushing."

Oh, how I hate the autonomic nervous system. "I don't know what you mean," I lied.

"Now you're going all Scarlett O'Hara on me, and that is even more worrying," she said. "So spill it."

I wouldn't let just any tech talk to me that way, but this was Ellie, who had never let me down. If anyone at the clinic had earned the right to shoot straight with me, it was her. "Uh...I had a lovely date."

"With the priest?"

"Yes," I said. "And the priest has a name—Jack."

"Do you, like, pray together?" she asked.

"What? No!" I said. "Don't be silly."

"I don't know why it's silly. My Uncle Bob is a Methodist pastor, and he and his wife pray together."

"First off, I am nobody's wife. And second...I'm not sure I believe in God."

"Does Father Jack know that?" Ellie asked.

"Please don't call him that," I sighed. "I don't know what to make of the whole priest thing."

"Were you ever religious?" Ellie asked.

"I was raised Catholic," I said. "I guess I'm what you call lapsed."

"Because?" she asked.

I shrugged. "I don't know. When I got to college, science seemed...a lot more knowable, I suppose. Religion has...too much mystery."

"That's what I like about it," Ellie said.

"I didn't know you were religious."

It was her turn to shrug. "I'd say I'm more spiritual. I don't go to church or anything. But I believe there's an energy force that moves through us and loves us and wants us to be kind to each other."

"That's lovely," I said, hoping it didn't sound too patronizing. "I kind of wish I believed that, too."

"What stops you?" She asked.

"Have you ever studied horse anatomy?" I asked. "No way an intelligent loving being put that monstrosity together. Poor horses."

"I have no idea what you're talking about," she said. "Anyway, I hope you give the good Father a chance."

"I hope I am. I mean...have you seen his lips?"

Ellie grinned and looked like she was going to punch me in the arm. She didn't, though.

Just then Ajeet came around the corner, and his big brown eyes lit up when he saw me. "Oh, Dr. Casey! Just the person I was hoping to speak with."

"Just so long as you don't want copies," Ellie moved away, back toward the reception area and her desk.

I turned to face him. "Yes, Ajeet? What's up?"

"I wanted to talk to you about my idea," he said.

Ajeet was a fountain of ideas, I had discovered. Most of them were—how shall I put this?—weird. "Which idea was that?"

"I'd like to start a Toenail Club." He grinned. It was a hopeful grin.

"A Toenail Club," I repeated, hoping it would make more sense if I said it aloud.

"Oh, yes. A Toenail Club."

The repeating didn't actually help much, I discovered. "Uh...okay, I'll bite. What's a Toenail Club?"

"One of the most difficult things we deal with every day is... what?" he asked.

I rolled my eyes. I did not really feel like playing guessing games. "Canine flatulence?" I asked.

"That is annoying, but not difficult," he said.

"Speak for yourself. I've been thinking of outfitting the exam rooms with gas masks."

"No," he said. "One of the hardest things we deal with is cutting the toenails of dogs."

That was true. Dogs in general hate having their toenails cut. Some got so vicious we actually had to anesthetize them just to do proper paw grooming. And it wasn't like cutting their nails was optional—uncut toenails could lead to serious paw problems. "I'm listening," I said.

"So we put out the word to our client list that once a week we're going to have Toenail Club. People can bring their dogs, and we'll do exercises together that will help their dogs become desensitized to having their toenails cut."

I blinked. It was an intriguing idea. "What kind of exercises?"

"Well, we start by teaching the owners to massage their dogs' paws—that gets the dogs used to having their paws touched and also creates a pleasurable association with it. Simple exercises like that, which will help the dogs be less anxious and resistant when they come in for a toenail trim." He grinned, showing me his impossibly white, impossibly straight teeth.

"That...actually sounds like a fine idea," I admitted. "Talk with Ellie to set up a time and an email blast and let's give it a try."

"Thank you, Casey!" He said, grabbing my hand and pumping it with excitement. Then he headed for the break room without another word.

"Toenail Club," I said to the copier.

Ellie knocked on the wall to get my attention. "Yes?" I said.

"Uh...your 11:00am is here. New client."

"Okay, thanks." I finished up at the copier and grabbed the nearly empty file from the rack. I let myself into Exam Room Two and was surprised to see a woman, but no animal. And then I recognized the woman—but from where? I'm terrible at recognizing people out of context, and it must have showed. The woman cleared her throat and looked nervous.

"Hello, Doctor, I'm Betty Swann. We met a couple days ago at...when my..." She looked down.

Then it hit me. "Oh, yes," I said, taking the seat next to her, and putting my hand on her knee. "You lost your dog. I'm so sorry. I'm afraid in all the hubbub—"

"No need to apologize, it was...a pretty confusing time."

Her eyes were moist, and she looked around. I jumped up and snatched a box of tissues off the shelf and put them on the metal examination table within her easy reach.

"Your German Shepherd was named Anselm," I recalled. Jack had given me a whole lecture on a St. Anselm all the way home from the dog show, which interested me not at all, but I knew he was trying to take my mind off the troubling events of the day.

"Yes. He was...a beautiful boy. The best..." She grabbed at a tissue and held it to her face. I waited patiently for the emotion to pass.

"He was a very pretty dog," I agreed. "Was he a champion?"

"Oh, yes." She lowered the tissue and for a brief moment I saw the pride on her face.

"Do you know what happened to him?" I asked.

"His handler—"

"Mr. Teal?" I recalled.

"Yes. Austin. He was lovely. I was in no shape to...well, to do much of anything. And Austin just stepped in and...handled things. He sent Anselm's body to a vet he works closely with for the autopsy—"

"Necropsy," I corrected her.

"What?" she asked.

"Never mind," I waved it away. "Have you gotten the results back yet?"

"No, but...that's why I'm here. Austin is going to send me the vet's report, and I...well, I don't imagine I'll be able to make heads or tails of it. I was wondering if maybe...since you were there...since you—well, you didn't know him, but you *saw* him

—maybe if you'd help me decipher it...help me understand what happened to him?"

"Of course, but...what about your regular vet?"

"He just retired and...well, I don't much like the person who took over for him. She's...well, best not speak ill of people. I'm looking for a *new* vet. Let's just leave it there."

"Do you have other animals?" I asked, making a few notes in the folder.

"I have one other Shepherd, Abelard."

"Do you show Abelard?"

"Oh, yes. He's just got his championship."

"I look forward to seeing him at his next checkup." I gave her a compassionate smile.

"I'll bring him in just as soon as his shows are over. He's with Austin now. There's a show in San Diego next week, then Tijuana, and then Mexicali."

"Quite the international dog," I said.

"Yes," she said. "And he's doing so well."

"I'm glad to hear it. A dog who does well in the ring wins security. It's not something every dog has."

"I've never thought of that," Betty said, "but I suppose you're right."

"Well, Ms. Swann, I'd be delighted to be your new vet. We'll have some paperwork for you—you can pick it up at the desk. And you can email me the report when you get it," I handed her my card. "I'll call you the same day I get it to talk you through it. If we're busy, it might be after supper, but I'll call as soon as I can manage it. I promise."

"Doctor, I'm so glad I came. I've been so anxious since Anselm was...died."

I picked up on the hitch in her sentence. "Do you...suspect something?"

"It's not normal for a dog to foam at the mouth and just collapse, is it?"

"No, it's not normal, but there are a number of conditions that can present that way."

"Oh. It just didn't seem..." She looked flustered.

"You think someone killed Anselm?" I asked.

She nodded. "I do. He sweeps every showing he's in, and... and there are a lot of other owners who would just rather he wasn't there, you know?"

That was troubling. Dog show people can be obsessive—I know, because I have been one of those people. But to murder a dog...that was a line I couldn't imagine any dog lover crossing. "Do you have someone in mind?"

"Yes, but..." She looked away, her eyes fixing on a framed Norman Rockwell painting of a vet at work. "But let's see what the autopsy report says before we point any fingers, shall we?"

I nodded. "That seems wise. Do you have any idea when you'll get it?"

"Austin says any day now. But as soon as I get it, I'll forward it immediately."

I placed my hand on her arm. "Good. And take care of yourself. Our culture discourages us from taking our feelings about pets too seriously. But I can see that you loved Anselm. That love was real, and it was big. Don't feel bad for being sad right now."

She nodded and grasped my hand. "Thank you. Thank you so much."

I closed the folder and stood, holding the door for her. I closed it after her and sighed. I couldn't imagine how I would feel if it had been Scout who had died in front of me. On the other hand, I had a pretty good idea. I'd be devastated.

five

I told Scout to stay by the door of Millie's Diner. She lay down and put her head on her front paws, looking up at me with the saddest eyes she could manage.

"Don't give me that. I'm bringing you leftovers." This did not seem to mollify her, but I swung open the door to the diner anyway. I headed straight for one of the stools at the counter.

"Hey, Case," a voice called. I whipped my head around and saw Gus waving at me.

"Hey, Gus," I returned with a wave.

I slid onto a stool and put my elbows on the counter just as Sarge came through the swinging doors from the kitchen. "Hello, Doctor," he said with a welcoming grin. Sarge was half again my height, with bulging muscles that threatened to tear the sleeves of his t-shirt. His skin was so dark it was hard to see the outlines of his tattoos.

"Hi, Sarge. How's Prince?" Prince was Sarge's Cavalier King Charles Spaniel, who spent the time when Sarge was at work in a cushy run behind the diner.

"Oh, he's fine, fine. Getting a little chubby, maybe."

Without asking he poured a cup of coffee and put it in front of me.

"If you'd stop feeding him béarnaise sauce, he'd be healthier," I said.

"But then I'd have to face his wrath. Hard to disappoint my pretty boy."

I tasted the coffee. I made a face. "Ugh...how old is this?"

"Oh...uh...couple hours, maybe."

I pushed the cup away. "You know what? I think I'll have a glass of wine."

"Wine it is. What kind?"

"Your best boxed red?" I cringed.

"Ha! I can do you one better. I just opened a Napa Valley cabernet a half hour ago, and it's had a chance to breathe. How about that?"

"You are a lifesaver."

Sarge grabbed a wine glass and filled it halfway with the cab. He set it down in front of me. Under his breath, he said, "He's staring at you, you know." I started to turn, but Sarge put his hand up. "Don't move."

"Who's staring at me?" I asked.

"Deputy Gus. Can't take his eyes off you."

I sighed. "I know. He has a crush on me."

"He sure does. Have you encouraged him?"

"No!" I protested. "And it's not like he doesn't know I'm dating Jack."

Sarge shook his head. "The heart wants what it wants."

I intuited that that statement applied to Sarge more than Gus. "How did you survive in the army without...you know... being out of the closet?"

He shrugged. "I just stayed in the closet. I wasn't alone. A lot of us felt it was worth it to serve our country."

"Didn't you ever get...lonely?"

"Oh, yeah. Powerful lonely. But it was only twenty years—"

"Twenty years!"

"—and we got vacations. It's not like I didn't get to play."

"But you didn't get to have a real partner," I said.

He shrugged again. "Still don't."

"Do you want it that way?"

"Some days I don't...other days, I realize just how set in my ways I am."

I nodded. I had been feeling the same. A part of me desperately wanted things with Jack to progress, while another part was afraid of losing the life I had.

"You gonna eat something?" he asked.

"Oh, yeah. Uh...what's the special?"

"Mexican shepherd's pie—only with mashed butternut squash instead of potatoes."

"Oh. That...sounds amazing. Yes, please."

"It has a bit of spice to it," he warned.

"Probably not enough. Bring me the Tapatío sauce too, please."

"That's my girl," he laughed. He turned to face the window into the kitchen. "Special with a side of pickled jalapeños." He turned back and winked at me.

"Perfect," I said. Just then my phone rang. "Sorry," I said to Sarge. He waved my apology away and picked up his coffee pot to make the rounds of the other customers.

"Hello," I said.

"Casey, this is Betty, Betty Swann."

"Oh, Ms. Swann. I'm so glad you called. Did you get the report?"

"I did. I forwarded it to your email. Could you...take a look?"

"Sure." I put the phone on speaker and opened my email

app. The message from Betty was right on top, and I tapped on the attachment. I turned my phone sideways to get a better look at it. It was a standard necropsy report—but it wasn't complete. It was just the gross post—the histopathology and toxicology sections were missing. That didn't surprise me, as those usually take longer to come through. What did surprise me, however, was that there was already a conclusion in the summary. "Natural causes?" I exclaimed. "What the actual—" I stopped myself before I swore in front of a client.

"That's the only thing I could understand…and I don't understand that." Betty's voice was tinny coming from the tiny speaker.

"Betty, I was there. There was nothing natural about that death."

"I didn't think it could be," she said.

"Did they send a histopathology or toxicology report?" I asked.

"No. I know what a toxicology report is," she said, "but what is a histo-histo—"

"Histopathology," I rescued her. "It's a microscopic examination of tissues."

"Oh. Okay."

"Ms. Swann, this report isn't complete. We're missing two-thirds of it. Maybe they just forgot—unlikely. Maybe they got lost in cyberspace—also unlikely, since they usually put it all on one form if they have the information. Most likely is that your vet is sending you what they have, and more is coming. I recommend you call the vet yourself to check up on this—the number is on the form."

"Austin wouldn't like me going around him."

"Screw Aus—sorry, Betty. Anselm was your dog, not Austin's. You have to be responsible for him."

"You're right. I know you're right."

I was beginning to get the feeling that Austin Teal was a bit of an intimidating personality. Well, he wouldn't intimidate me. "Call the vet and ask them to resend the histopathology and toxicology sections of the report. And if by chance they didn't run them, order it."

"If it's a normal part of the report, why wouldn't they run them?"

"Well..." I sighed. "I don't know your Mr. Teal, but if he's paying for this report—and he should, since the dog was in his care when this happened—but if he's paying, he might have only ordered the gross post to save money. The fact that they rendered a summary without the other parts on board makes me suspect that's what's up."

"Oh."

I could hear the disappointment in her voice, and I sympathized. "If that's true, it's a lousy thing to do," I told her. "So call. Can you do it today?"

"They're closed now, but I'll do it tomorrow."

"Good. In the meantime, I'll study this when I get home and will let you know if I come up with anything."

"Thank you, Dr. Gibbons."

I hung up just as Sarge was replacing the coffee pot. "I know that look," Sarge said.

"General annoyance?" I asked.

"Is that what that is?"

"I think so," I said, sipping at the wine. The complex flavors blossomed in my mouth.

"Dare I ask?"

I sighed and then told him about the dog show and its ignominious end. He whistled. "What a mess."

"You can say that again. The dog's owner suspects one of the owners of the competing dogs."

"Does she know which owner could'a done it?"

"That's a good question," I said. "But it's a question for tomorrow."

six

The next morning I had a 9am appointment, but I hung back long enough to give Betty Swann a call. "Dr. Casey, good morning," she said.

"Have you called the vet yet to ask about the missing reports?" I asked without preamble. I'm terrible at small talk. Ask anyone.

"Oh...uh...they were supposed to be open at eight, so I left a message. I haven't heard back yet."

"I wish I didn't have to say that you might need to pester them...but you might need to pester them."

"I can do that," she said. "But..."

"But what?" I suddenly realized I had been in full business mode and had not really been listening to her. She was stuttering and hesitant. She sounded rattled. "Ms. Swann, is there something wrong?"

"I—I saw something on Facebook this morning, and I'm..."

"What? What did you see?"

"Someone posted a picture of my Anselm, when he was

dying..." Her voice pitched higher, and I knew she was about to cry.

"Oh. Oh, my. I'm so sorry you had to see that again."

She snuffled and let out a woeful squeak. When she regained her composure, she said, "But that's not the worst."

"What...what could be worse?"

"She wrote 'Good Riddance.'"

"Do you recognize the person who posted?" I asked.

"Yes...she has a Shepherd named Bully. Anselm always beat him in the ring."

"Egad." I didn't know what else to say.

"But...some of the responses are even worse. One of them, especially—and that one is from another dog that Anselm always beat out. Do you...do you think maybe...one of them could have poisoned him?"

"I don't know," I said. "But it's possible. That's why we need that toxicology report."

"Of course."

"Betty, is your Facebook page under your name?"

"Yes."

"Okay. I'll take a look as soon as I have a spare moment."

"That would be great."

"I'll talk to you soon."

"Dr. Casey...thank you for caring so much."

"No problem," I said. "Please call me if you hear anything else, and if I can't pick up, please leave a message. No one will hear but me."

"Of course. Thank you."

I hung up and turned to see Ellie coming out of the bathroom. Keeping my voice low, I sidled up to her and said, "Can you check out Betty Swann's Facebook page? She said someone posted a picture of her dog dying. We think her dog was poisoned, and it might be one of the more spiteful posters who did it."

"Betty with an 'e' at the end, or a 'y'?" Ellie asked.

"With a 'y'—oh, and Swann has a double 'n.'"

"On it," she said. Just then Stacy ran around the corner in a frenzied rush. "Possible stroke, elderly Newfoundland bitch— Exam Room Two."

"Yikes," I said involuntarily. I immediately headed for Two.

"I'll bring you the file," Stacy said.

"Thank you," I said as I turned the knob to the room.

It was a Newfoundland, all right, which meant she was bigger than I was. She was certainly bigger than her owner, a pale, wan woman in her middle forties. Her eyes were red from crying, and her hands shook. She looked up at me pleadingly as I knelt by her dog.

"I'm Dr. Gibbons," I said. "You must have been one of Dr. Capra's clients."

"Yes. I heard she died. I'm...sorry."

"What is your name?" Where was Stacy with that file? It was embarrassing to have to ask such questions.

"Avis Browne. And this is Sheila."

"How long has Sheila been like this?"

"I just came downstairs this morning and she was like this."

"Can she stand?" I asked.

"No."

"How did you get her here?" There was no way this woman could have lifted this dog.

"My husband carried her in."

"Where is he?" I asked.

"In the waiting room. He can't watch. He's...he's too upset."

"Okay, I understand."

The dog's eyes were open, but she was whining. Her head was on the ground, and every now and then she tried to lift it, but it seemed to be lying at an odd angle. She tried to roll but couldn't get over.

"It's a stroke, isn't it?"

"It could be," I said.

"Oh, God, I knew it. My baby..."

I pulled out my pen light and, holding one eye open, I shone the light in the bitch's eye. It twitched back and forth. I looked at the other eye—it was the same. I breathed a sigh of relief, and felt my shoulders relax. Just for due diligence, I completed my exam. Then I sat back on the floor cross-legged and stroked the dog's fur reassuringly. "It's okay, girl. You're going to be all right."

"She is?" the woman asked, her voice cracking.

"Yes. Why don't you call your husband in here, tell him it's good news, and I'll explain."

"Okay." But she didn't move, didn't take her hand off her dog.

"It's okay. I'll sit here with Sheila. She isn't going anywhere just yet."

"Okay," she said again. On shaky legs she rose and opened the door into the waiting room. "Alan?"

A moment later, a burly man with a large pot belly entered the room. His eyes, too, were red and he looked stricken. "Hi, Alan," I said. "I'm Dr. Gibbons. Please have a seat."

"Is she going to die?" he asked.

"Not today," I said. "Not anytime soon, from the looks of her."

They continued to stand, holding onto each other. I really wished they'd sit down. I patted the floor beside their dog. "Come and put your hands on Sheila. She needs the reassurance."

That did it. They both sat on the floor, and instantly began to stroke the massive beast. A whine escaped her lips, but it seemed like a good whine.

"It is possible that she's had a stroke...but it isn't likely. I think what is troubling Sheila here is Old Dog Vestibular Disease. These days we call it Idiopathic Vestibular Disease, but I'm set in my ways."

"What does that mean?" Alan asked.

"It means that something in her inner ear is messed up, and she has lost her sense of balance. If she doesn't lie down, she'll fall down. So, like the smart girl she is, she is staying on the floor so that the room doesn't spin quite so fast."

"Is it serious?" Avis asked.

"No, thank God," I said. "No one knows why it happens, but it's not uncommon in older dogs. The good news is that it usually passes in a couple of days."

"What causes it?" Alan asked.

"No one knows," I said. "That's why they call it 'idiopathic.'"

He nodded. "So what do we do?"

I pulled my prescription pad out of my lab coat pocket and clicked my pen. "I'm going to give you a prescription for some pretty powerful anti-nausea medication. We'll give her a shot for the first dose, but then you should be able to pill her—do you know how to do that?"

"Yes. She takes pills," Alan said.

"Good. Now she'll take another one...but not for long—just a week or so. I'll give you a two-week supply, but you can stop as soon as she's up and walking around again. The most important thing is to comfort her and keep her hydrated. This is a very traumatic event for Sheila, so the more attention and love and petting you can give her in the next couple of days, the better. And she's going to have trouble drinking, so I recommend going to the pet store and getting one of those large water bottles with the little ball at the end of the metal spout—"

"Like with hamsters?" Avis asked.

"Exactly like the hamsters have," I said, "only bigger. Then you can hold it to her lips and she can drink. Every hour or so. And you'll need to help her stand up to go pee. In fact, it's probably a good idea to put down some of those large diaper-type absorbent pads so she can just go where she is, although she might not do it—she looks like a good girl and will really want to go out to go potty."

They nodded. "She'll really be okay?" Alan asked, his voice squeaking with tearful relief.

"In my expert opinion, she'll be up and shedding hair all over your house again in a few days."

I rose, ignoring my creaking knee. "Thank you, doctor," Avis said.

"My pleasure." I handed her the prescription.

"Ellie will be in soon to give her a shot. Please call me if she doesn't improve in a few days."

They nodded, looking relieved and hopeful and shell-shocked, all at once. I let myself out through the room's rear door and leaned against the hallway wall, blowing air through my cheeks in relief. "Thank God for the easy ones," I said.

I walked up to the reception area to enter my notes and drop off the file folder. Ellie waved me over to her station. I put one hand on the back of her chair, and the other on her desk, leaning over her shoulder to get a good look at her screen. "What did you find?"

"Here's Betty Swann's Facebook page. There's no picture of her dog on her page, but I suspect that's because Ms. Swann doesn't understand how Facebook works. How old is she?"

I narrowed one eye at her. "No older than I am," I said testily.

"Right, so you understand what I mean." I rolled my eyes as she continued. "I found a post that probably showed up in Betty's feed, because she'd been tagged." Her fingers flew over the keyboard, and a post popped up on her screen. I recoiled at the sight of it. It was of Anselm, eyes wide with fright, foaming at the mouth, his legs blurred and stuck out at odd angles, mid-twitch. Above the photo were the words, "Anselm—good riddance. Rest in hell."

"I can't believe human beings sometimes." I thought of the dictum about academic life—that the politics were so vicious because the stakes were so small—and realized it was doubly true of the dog show world.

"Check this out," Ellie said, scrolling down to the comments below the photo.

Most were the social media equivalent of cackling, but one wrote. "That show was rigged. The title was stolen from my dog Peppy. It was about time someone did something."

"Who are these people?" I asked.

Ellie handed me a stack of paper. "I checked out the home pages of the two worst offenders. I've printed out several of their posts. You might want to liquor up before you read them."

"Thanks for the warning," I said, taking the papers but feeling like I needed to hold them at arm's length as if they were odiferous fish. "Are they using aliases?"

"No, strangely. They're using their real names. And they don't live far." She handed me another sheet of paper. "Here are their addresses."

I took the paper absently and put it on top of the stack. I looked at Ellie with something akin to wonder. "You are a goddess," I said.

"I think of myself as more of a demigod, like Hercules. You know, awe-inspiring, but not omnipotent."

"Fair enough," I agreed.

"So...what are you going to do with this information?" Ellie asked. That was a good question, and one that I didn't know the answer to. Before I could say anything, Ellie thought out loud. "I mean, it's good to know who might have hurt this dog, and where they live. But...what are you going to do about it?"

"I could take it to the police," I said.

"Do you think they'll care?" Ellie asked.

"Surely murdering a dog is a crime," I said, not at all sure that it was.

"I don't know," Ellie said. "But I'll bet you know someone who would love to tell you."

seven

When I got home that night, I rooted around in the top drawer of my chest of drawers for Gus' card. My top drawer is a "catch-all" drawer where I throw anything that I'm too lazy to put away properly, so it took some time. Eventually, though, I found it—creased and stained with what looked like grease, but readable.

Scout was leaping around like a jumping bean, wanting attention and dinner—probably not in that order.

"Hold your horses," I told her and dialed Gus' cell phone. Scout whined and turned in circles. A few moments later, she left the room. In the distance I heard the dog door to the back yard clack as it closed behind her.

It rang twice before Gus picked up. "Tucker," he said.

"Gus?" I asked.

"Casey?" His voice cracked as he said my name. It was adorable.

"Yeah, it's me. Hey, can I pick your brain for a moment?"

"Sure. Let me pull over." I heard the ambient noise on the other end of the line quiet down, and then a couple of loud clicks. Then Gus' voice, clearer than before, said, "Okay. What can I do for you?"

"Are you still on duty?" I asked.

"No, I'm on my way home," he said.

"Good. I don't want to take you away from your work." Why was I beating around the bush? Talking to Gus made me nervous for some reason. I cleared my throat and got down to business. "I think someone murdered one of my clients' dogs."

"Oh? How?"

"Well, I don't know for certain yet, but I think he was poisoned."

"Oh. That's terrible."

"Well, it is. I watched the dog die. It isn't something I ever want to see again."

"Geez, Case, I'm so sorry."

"I'm sure you see worse in your line of work."

"I do have to peel what's left of wild turkeys off the pavement."

"It's a tough job, but someone's got to do it," I joked.

"Damn straight. What's your question?"

"Oh, right. Uh...so is it illegal to kill someone's dog?"

"It is," Gus said. "There's a couple of ways you can approach it. First, under California state law, killing a dog is felony abuse and you can get three years or a $20,000 fine, or both. Or, you could go federal and report it to the FBI. Then it would be handled as an unreasonable seizure of property."

"What if I can't get anyone to pay attention?" I asked.

"You mean, if you can't get law enforcement to act?" he asked.

"Yes."

"You don't have high regard for us, do you?"

"I'm being realistic. We're talking about a dog."

"I wish you weren't right, but...you're right. It would have to be a pretty slow week for the sheriff to assign anyone to something like this."

"So? What do I do if I can't get you badges off your butts?"

"You could sue in civil court."

I blinked. That was exactly what Maggie Edgerton was doing to me—suing me for the unlawful death of her dog. Shelley had actually done the surgery, but Shelley was dead, so now I was the target. It felt too close to home. "I'll keep that in my back pocket," I said.

"Casey, anything else I can do?"

"I don't think so, Gus. You've been a great help."

"Because we could meet up at Millie's to brainstorm this anytime, and...I don't know...have some pie?"

I smiled, closed my eyes, and shook my head. I had to hand it to him. He did not give up easy. "I'll keep that in mind, Gus. Thank you so much."

"No problem. You take care now," he said.

"Seeya." I hung up. I heard a bark. I turned toward Scout. "I have not forgotten about you."

She didn't look sure.

"Let's get you some dinner," I said, and we headed for the kitchen.

eight

The next morning was a whirlwind of activity. It was a surgery day, and I'd found two corks literally stopping up the plumbing of a Rottweiler named Sammy. I met his owner for a debrief and discovered she was a winemaker and had boxes of corks just lying around in her basement. "Put them on a high shelf when you're not bottling," I informed her. "Otherwise, you'll be laying down this dog rather than a Merlot—and Rottweilers don't age well." I gave her the stink eye as I said this, and she looked properly chagrined.

I dropped the file off at the front desk only to find the place in a bit of an uproar. Stacy was shouting at someone across the counter, "No appointment, no meeting!"

"But I—" a voice protested. I recognized that voice. I angled around to where I could view the waiting room and saw Betty Swann in what looked like bunny slippers and a winter coat.

"What's going on?" I asked.

"This woman insists on meeting with you, but she doesn't have an appointment and we're booked up."

She was right about the booked-up part—the waiting room was full, and nobody looked happy, especially the St. Bernard that looked ready to hurl.

"It's okay, Stacy, this is an emergency," I said. "It'll take me five minutes, tops. Do we have an open room?" I had no idea how long it would take, but I had to manage the situation somehow before it escalated into a catfight.

"No, we don't have an open room!" Stacy snapped.

I lifted up a section of the counter so Betty could pass. "We'll be in the break room," I said to the staff. "Give us our privacy for five minutes."

I waved Betty through and pointed to the door to the break room. As I followed her, I heard Stacy ask someone, "What, are they lesbians?"

I rolled my eyes and shut the door. "Have a seat."

There was half a box of Girl Scout cookies on the table—peanut butter Do-Si-Dos. I wiped the crumbs off the plastic tablecloth and sat across from her. "I don't have much time. What's up?"

"I'm sorry—"

"It's okay. Just tell me what happened."

"I heard from the vet about the autopsy—"

"Necropsy," I corrected.

"—report," she finished. "You were right, Austin only ordered the-the-the physical whatsit—"

"The gross post," I offered.

"When I asked why, the girl at the clinic didn't know."

"And you haven't talked to Mr. Teal yet?" I asked.

"I left him a voicemail message...but no, not yet."

"So did you order the histopathology and toxicology reports?"

"I tried, but..." Her lower lip started to quiver.

"You tried, but what?" I asked.

"They don't have his body anymore." She buried her face in her hands and began to sob.

"What the hell?" I asked. Displays of emotion make me uncomfortable. But I had the good sense to wait for her sobs to subside. "Why don't they have his body?" I asked. "Where is it?"

"They cremated it," she said, although I could barely make out her words through the wailing.

I handed her a paper napkin from the holder on the table. She blew her nose. "On whose authority?" I asked.

"I don't know. On Austin's, I guess."

"But you didn't sign off on it?" I clarified.

"No, never. I have a place in the yard picked out for him. Now I guess I'll just have to put his ashes there. Oh, poor Anselm! He deserved so mush m..." But her words decayed into unintelligible squeaks.

"That's criminal," I said. "No, literally. It's against the law to do that. Only you get to decide that." I'm not sure what that bit of information was supposed to achieve. It didn't seem to comfort her at all. Also, I wasn't at all sure it was correct.

I looked at the clock on the wall. Our five minutes had passed. I could literally feel Stacy boring holes in the wall with her x-ray eyes. In mere seconds, she'd be pounding on the door demanding that I stand and deliver.

"Betty, look at me." She sniffed, wiped her nose, then looked up. Her eyes were swollen and red.

"Now we'll never know if he was poisoned or not," she said. Then she looked momentarily hopeful. "Can you test the ashes?"

I shook my head no. Her face fell again. "No. I thought not."

I stood and waited. She took the hint and stood too. "I'm so sorry, Betty. We're not going to give up, but...this is a setback for sure."

"Why would Austin do this?"

"I'm not sure. There are lots of reasons, though—a misunderstanding, expediency, cost, wrongly anticipating your wishes...you need to ask him."

"Yes. Yes, I need to ask him."

She moved toward the door like a zombie and let herself out. I followed and Stacy jabbed her index finger toward the rack with today's files in it. "Exam Room Two," she called. Wordlessly and mindlessly, I reached for the foremost file and headed for the room. All I could hear was Betty's voice ringing in my ears, *Now we'll never know if he was poisoned or not.* An answering voice in my head said, *Wanna bet?*

nine

I was seething for the rest of the day. The problem was, I didn't know who I was more pissed off at—Austin Teal or Betty's vet. Both were culpable, as far as I was concerned. Someone was responsible for Anselm's death, and I felt like a dog with a bone—I just couldn't let it go. Or maybe I should say it wouldn't let go of me. In any case, I was distracted all day. All I could see was Betty sobbing at our break table. The memory of her dog dying, twitching in a pool of foam, haunted me as well.

I was so absorbed that I seemed to come to only when I reached the parking lot. I had no memory of wrapping up, of filing my last set of notes, or of leaving the clinic. It was all a blur.

I hate being frustrated. I hate when I need something and can't get it. I needed to know what had killed Anselm, but his unauthorized cremation was a brick wall, and I had smashed right into it. The toxicology tests were certainly the best way I might have gotten that information, and now that option had been taken away. *How else can I find out?* I asked myself.

An idea formed in my head that I immediately pushed away. It was simply too dangerous. But I—

"What are you thinking about, boss?" Ellie asked.

"Wha—?" I turned and saw her standing behind me.

"You're pretty checked out there. Deep in uffish thought. What are you thinking about?"

I wondered if I dared share the crazy idea I'd just had. I decided against it. Instead, I described everything up to hitting the brick wall.

"Oh," she said. She looked at her shoes, her eyes moving back and forth as she thought. "You need another way of finding out what killed that dog."

"Yes," I said. "That's...what I was thinking about."

She nodded. "Well, you know, I gave you those addresses. You could do some snooping around. You might find something...incriminating."

She had just named the crazy idea. For some strange reason, that made it seem less crazy. "That's a crazy idea," I said.

She shrugged. "I don't see another way."

I didn't either. That was the problem. "How would I get the owners out of their houses long enough to...go snooping?" I wondered aloud.

For a few moments we stood there in silence. Then Ellie looked up, a broad smile on her face. "We send them an invitation—we make it seem like a big deal, like they've won something."

"What would they win?"

"A free class."

"What class?" I asked.

"Toenail Club," she said.

ten

I had to admit it was brilliant. The invitation to Toenail Club had gotten the owners out of their houses—along with their dogs—for a good couple of hours. I looked at the paper in my hand—the one Ellie had printed out with the names of Betty's most virulent online assailants. I looked up at the house. I was parked outside. All seemed quiet. The paper said it belonged to Jessica Sneed, owner of a German Shepherd named Andy. Andy had consistently come in second and third in his class—always behind Anselm.

I looked around at the other houses in the neighborhood. I saw no one. If anyone was watching, I couldn't see them. I put a crowbar under my coat and got out of my car. I kept my head down and did not look around. I let myself in by the side gate and went directly to the back door. The sun was going down; the backyard was overgrown with weeds. The scent of fennel was both overwhelming and intoxicating. I snatched a pair of blue nitrile gloves from my pocket and put them on. Then I tried the back door. It was locked, but there was a dog door. I pushed it in to see if the inner door had been slid over it—the flap waved back and forth unhindered. "Huh," I said to myself. "That seems way too easy." I flopped onto my knees and put my head through the dog door.

I've never given my height much thought, but I had to admit that being a short woman on the petite side definitely came with advantages when it came to breaking and entering. German Shepherds are not small dogs, and it didn't take much effort to squeeze my shoulders and hips through the dog door. I reached back through and snagged the crowbar, just in case I met with any surprises.

I turned on the light in the kitchen, put the crowbar on the counter and began my search. I looked under the sink, all the while doing an inventory in my head of all the substances that might have the effect that I saw on Anselm the day he died. I had done some research on the matter and was pretty well-versed. There were some cleaning agents that could do it, some pesticides, and some pharmaceuticals.

Checking under the sink, I saw lots of chemical agents, but none that would have had that exact effect. I did a quick search of the drawers and found nothing there either. There was a laundry room with a utility sink—I envied that. I checked the cupboards but came up empty. It was obviously where Sneed kept the dog stuff, but I didn't see anything that might have poisoned Anselm, not even in Sneed's dog travel kit. That disappointed me. All dog owners that do shows have a duffle bag that holds all their show paraphernalia. I had hoped that I'd find the poison there. But no. I found grooming supplies, leashes, poop bags, a travel water bowl, and treats, but that was about it.

"Damn," I said. I explored further afield. I found the garage and turned on the light. I started checking cupboards and found snail-and-slug pellets. I paused but realized that wasn't quite right—it would poison a dog, all right, but it would take longer and there would be severe and extended convulsions leading up to death. It simply wasn't consistent with what I'd seen.

I had just shut the cupboard door when I heard a car door slam just outside the garage. "Damn," I breathed. I looked around quickly and saw that there was a door in the garage leading to the side yard. I was about to open it when I remembered the crowbar. It had my fingerprints on it, and it was sitting on the kitchen counter.

I turned and ran back into the house, around the corner, into the kitchen. I grabbed the crowbar, nearly knocking a pepper-grinder to the floor. I ran for the garage again, turning off lights as I went. Just before I opened the door, I stopped and took a deep breath, steadying myself. I put the crowbar under my coat again. Then I turned the knob. I jumped when I saw a man blocking my way. He shone a flashlight in my face. I squinted and held my free hand up to block the light.

"Casey," Gus's voice said. "What in the world are you doing here?"

eleven

The interrogation room looked just like it did on TV—cinderblock walls painted an industrial gray, a metal table with uncomfortable metal chairs. A double-sided mirror took up most of one wall, directly facing me. Pole-length fluorescent lights bathed the room in antiseptic blue light. It was cold. I hugged myself to try to keep warm, wishing I had a sweater.

After what seemed like an eternity, Gus entered through the only door. For a moment, he just stood in the doorway, scowling.

"Stop that," I said. "You remind me of my mother."

He didn't say anything. Instead, he shut the door behind him and sat in one of the metal chairs across the table from me. He met my eyes and said, "Casey, this is bad."

"Was anything missing?" I asked.

"What?"

"I said, was anything missing? From the house?"

"No," he said.

"You've checked with the owners?"

"Yes. Nothing is missing."

"Was there any damage to the property?" I asked.

Gus blinked, looking confused. "Uh...no."

"No," I said. "No damage. What's the worst they can do to me?"

"You're not taking this seriously," Gus said.

"Wrong," I countered. "I'm taking this very seriously. I'm just trying to be realistic. You are not going to charge me with burglary—I didn't steal anything. You're not going to charge me with vandalism—I didn't damage anything. So what are you going to charge me with?"

"The sheriff and the ADA...haven't decided yet."

"What's the worst that could happen?"

"$1000 fine, up to six months in jail. Probation."

I shrugged. "Bring it on." In truth, I was squirming in my seat, but I didn't want Gus to know that.

He ran his fingers through his hair. "Jeez, Case. I really don't understand you. What were you doing there?"

"Off the record or on?" I asked.

"Well, anything you say—"

"I'll keep my own counsel, then," I said.

"I just didn't take you for—"

"For what? Someone who puts herself in danger in order to help someone else?"

He stopped with his mouth open, clearly flummoxed. "Wha...? Is that what you were doing? How were you helping someone?"

I sighed. What could it hurt? The truth was always the best. I gave in. "Do you remember when I asked you about the penalty for killing a dog?"

A look of concern clouded his face. "Yeah. What does that have to do—"

I ignored him and pressed on. "That dog I was telling you

about, the one I saw die—I think he was poisoned. But the body was destroyed before I could get a toxicology report."

"By who?"

"I think you mean 'whom,'" I said, hating myself for being the grammar police. "A couple of local people had been posting threatening messages online—really bad stuff."

"Why didn't you report it?"

"Really, Gus? Someone says 'Your dog should die' on Facebook, and you fellas do *what* about it?"

Gus looked down at the table. "Not much."

"No. I didn't think so." I sighed. "I went into that house looking for evidence...for some kind of poison...anything that might help me tie those...horrible people who posted those things to the death of this dog."

Gus nodded, staring blankly at the table. "There was more than one?"

"Only one dog," I said.

"No, I mean...you said 'people,' like there was more than one person threatening this dog."

"Yeah."

"So...did you break into the other house earlier? Or were you going to break into it after you finished at the house you were...caught at?"

I opened my mouth, but before any words could come out the door swung open again and Fuchsia Carhart breezed in. "Not another word," she said. "And I want some time alone with my client."

Gus met my eye and gave me a curt nod. Then without a word he stood up and left the room. Fuchsia set her briefcase on the desk, opened it, and took out a yellow legal pad and a pen. Then she set a Diet Coke on the desk in front of her and another can in front of me. I reached for it. It was still cold from the machine.

"You know, when I said, 'Let's grab a drink sometime,' this was not what I had in mind," Fuchsia said. A nervous, involuntary chuckle escaped my throat, but there was no humor in Fuchsia's face. She pulled the metal chair back and it screeched on the linoleum. She sat in it and opened her can.

"Sorry," I said, and it sounded even lamer than I thought it would. "Did you call Jack?"

"I did. He checked in on your dog. She's fine."

"Did he feed her?"

"I didn't ask. Does he have a brain?"

"He does," I assured her.

"Let's assume he knows that dogs have to eat, then."

I hadn't given Jack a key. I didn't know how he'd get in. Perhaps he'd feed Scout through the fence? She could get out to the yard through the dog door. Fuchsia was right. I needed to trust Jack.

She clicked the end of her pen. "Okay. Explain."

So I did. I told her the whole story, from the day at the dog show to the present moment. Fuchsia's face was a blank sheet the whole time. I kept looking for some sort of reaction, but there was none. When I finished, she said, "That's it?"

"I was planning to break into another house, too, but I didn't get that far."

"That's just great," she said, jotting that down. "Do the police know that?"

I felt heat rise up my neck and I thought back to how my conversation with Gus had ended. "Not...for sure."

"Do they suspect? How?"

"I might have mentioned that there was more than one person making threats."

"So it's an inference?"

"Yes."

"We can handle that," she said, taking more notes.

"How bad is it?" I asked.

"Have you ever been arrested before?" she asked.

"Student protests," I said. "You know."

"That's okay, then. Did you do any time?" she asked.

"No," I said.

"Probation?"

"No."

"Okay, that's lucky." She set down her pen. Then she just stared at me.

"Do I have spinach in my teeth?" I asked.

"What?"

I changed the subject. "So what now?"

"Now I go and bail you out, and you go home and get some sleep. Then we get a court date, and we hope for the best. With no priors to speak of, I'm hoping we can squeak by with a fine and some probation."

I nodded. It could be worse, the voice in my head said. Being no expert on the matter, I didn't argue with it.

"You know this is going to be bad for our other case, don't you?"

"What do you mean?" I asked.

"The Edgerton civil action against the clinic."

I felt a prick of panic in my chest. "How so?"

"The Gold Country Veterinary Clinic's leading veterinarian is a criminal. If she's guilty of breaking and entering, why not dog killing?"

"That's absurd," I said.

"It's all about the optics." She made a "V" with her fingers and pointed them at her eyes.

"Don't do that," I said. "It reeks of bad TV."

She stood. "Sit tight. I'll see you in about an hour...maybe a little more."

twelve

I t was three hours before I was released. I was literally shivering by the time I exited the county jail into the relative warmth of the early Gold Country evening. It felt wonderful.

I looked around and saw a hand waving. It was Jack. My shoulders relaxed and I breathed a sigh of relief. He was standing beside his olive-green Mini Cooper. I jogged toward him and was relieved to see both Scout and Tripod in the back seats. Jack caught me up in a hug and held me very tight for longer than normal. I squeezed him back and just let myself be held. I didn't want to admit that I was scared—but I was. I didn't want to admit that being arrested had been upsetting—but it was. Jack knew that, and he was letting me know it was okay without saying a word.

"How are you?" he asked, as he finally released me.

"Unharmed," I said, heading for the passenger side.

"That's the sort of nonanswer the bishop doesn't let me get away with," Jack said, opening his door and squeezing into the Cooper.

I got in and closed the door. Scout thrust her head into the front seat area and began to slobber all over my cheek. I gave her a rub and reached back to give Tripod a pet too. Then I leaned my head against the window.

"Tired?" Jack asked, starting the engine.

"Exhausted. I also really need a hot bath. I don't know why they keep it so outrageously cold in there."

"Do they?"

"You wouldn't believe it. Air conditioning at this time of year—seems like a waste of taxpayer dollars."

Jack narrowed an eye at me. "This seems an inappropriate time to mount one's high horse."

"I don't speak Episcopalian," I said. "English, please."

"You know exactly what I mean," he said. "Moral superiority is hard for felons to claim."

"Ouch," I winced. "But it was a misdemeanor."

"Thank God for that," Jack said. "And...sorry. I didn't mean to pile on. I'm just...I'm kind of in shock."

"You and me both."

"Casey, what were you thinking?"

I filled him in on what had happened with Betty Swann's dog Anselm. He had been there. He had seen it. I hoped he'd sympathize with the urgency I felt around it.

When I finished, he whistled. "So you broke in hoping to find...poison?"

"Or some other clue as to what happened to Anselm."

"Jeez," he said. "You really put yourself at a lot of risk."

"No kidding," I said, more sarcastically than I intended.

"And did you find anything?" he asked.

"No. But I only searched the first house, and I'd really only started that."

His back stiffened and he almost bumped his head on the

ceiling of the little car. "Please tell me you're not going to try this again."

"Relax. I learned my lesson," I said.

"You're not invincible. Or indestructible," he said, his voice softening. "People shoot trespassers up here."

I looked out the window. The sound of our dogs panting in the back seat was calming. "How did you get Scout?"

"I borrowed a couple of ladders," he said. "I went over one side of your fence with one, and down the other side with the other. Then I picked Scout up, put her on my shoulders, and did it again."

"You're lucky you didn't fall and break something—on both of you."

"High horse," he said.

I sighed. "Is this how it's going to be?"

"Is what how what's going to be?"

"I don't need my mother shaking her finger at me. I know I screwed up."

He was silent for a few moments, watching the road. Then he glanced back over at me. "You're right, Case. I'm sorry. I'm just...I'm as shook up about this as you are."

I reached over and took his hand. He squeezed it. "I'm sorry too. I'm sorry I did this...to me, to Scout, to you, to the clinic..."

"Do you want absolution?" he asked. I choked out a laugh. It felt good. "I am duly authorized," he added.

"I'll pass, Father," I said. "But thank you."

"You know, I didn't think about the clinic," Jack said. "Do you think...?"

"I don't know," I confessed. "But something tells me this could be very, very bad for business."

thirteen

The next day I went to work early, as it was a surgery day and I had some paperwork to catch up on before the busy-ness began. I was draggy—my extra cup of coffee was not doing the trick. To my surprise, Ellie was already there.

"You're here early," I said.

"I could say the same about you," she said. She looked at me as if she were trying to discern a pattern on my cheek.

"What?" I asked, touching my face.

"Are you okay?"

"Yeah. A little tired..."

"Uh-huh..."

I sighed. "Okay, what do you know?"

"I ran into Gus last night at Millie's. We...commiserated."

"About me."

"Sort of. Yeah. And then there was the newspaper this morning."

"Oy."

"Don't worry—it was in the legal notices. No one reads those except for old men with too much time on their hands."

That did not comfort me. I headed for the back room and reached up into my cubby to see if I had any mail or files or anything else I needed to tend to. To my surprise, there was a brown paper bag filling up most of the space. I pulled it down.

Ellie approached and leaned against the countertop. "You wanna tell me about it?"

"Not really."

"I am sort of involved," she said. "I gave you the addresses."

That was true. But if I was going to get into any trouble, I didn't want to drag Ellie into it as well. No one needed to know that she'd given me the addresses. Unless...

"Did you tell Gus that?" I asked.

"Need to know," she said, shaking her head.

"Thank God for that," I said.

"So did you find anything...you know, before you got nabbed?"

"I didn't get 'nabbed.'"

She raised her eyebrows and crossed her arms.

"No. I didn't find anything...not yet. I was...interrupted."

"By Gus."

"Yes."

"Damn."

"Tell me about it."

"Are you in any trouble?" she asked.

"How could I not be?"

"What sort of trouble?" she asked.

"I'm not sure yet," I said. "It depends on whether someone reports me to the disciplinary board of the AVMA. And then there's the misdemeanor—that will depend on whether Jessica Sneed decides to press charges."

"Oh, I wouldn't worry about that," Ellie said.

"Why not?" I asked, glancing through the small pile of junk mail I'd missed yesterday.

"Um...let's just say Ms. Sneed started a new hate campaign on Facebook last night."

"Against me?"

"Yeah."

I looked up at her and narrowed my eyes. She looked like a child who had just hidden a present for her mom. "What did you do?"

"Let's just say Ms. Sneed got an anonymous message documenting her hate speech and implicating her in the death of Anselm. The message also demonstrated the FB tags of everyone in the local German Shepherd Club. And let's just say that her threatening posts were deleted a short time later."

I blinked. "Ellie, that was...thank you." I froze as my thoughts whirred. "Do you think it's enough to dissuade her from..."

"Pressing charges?" she asked.

"Yeah."

She shrugged. "Here's hoping."

"Is there any way she can trace that back to you?"

Ellie shook her head. "She'd have to be a better hacker than I am."

"How do you know she isn't?"

"Her email is from an AOL account."

I laughed. She laughed. It felt good.

"What's this?" I pointed at the paper sack.

"It's not a bomb," Ellie said. "But you might wish it was."

I unrolled the top lip of the bag and peered inside. I caught sight of the gleam of what looked like white porcelain. I reached in and found what felt like a teapot. I pulled it out.

It was not a teapot—for one thing it was too small. And it was shaped wrong. It looked more like an Aladdin's lamp. "What is it?" I asked.

"I asked the same thing," she said.

"Of whom?"

"Of Ajeet."

I reached in and pulled forth several small packets of what might have been sugar. I peered at them to read the tiny print, which identified them as being filled with saline crystals. "What in the world?"

"Dr. Singh thought you looked stressed, so he gave you a neti pot."

"What in the hell is a neti pot?" I asked.

"I asked him that. He said that you put warm water in it, and then you put the spout up to your nostril, so that it makes a seal, then you lean your head sideways over a sink—and the warm water comes out the free nostril, along with a lot of goop."

"Ugh," I said. "Whyever for?"

She shrugged. "He said it was relaxing and that it cleared out some kind of negative jujus that I didn't understand. I think he used a Sanskrit word."

I peered inside the pot. There was some definite schmutz in it. "Is this a new neti pot, or a used neti pot?" I asked.

"He thought your need was urgent, so he gave you his. He said he'd get a new one. He said you can put it in the dishwasher."

I shuddered and, holding it by its handle as if it were a dead fish, I lowered it gently back into the paper bag. "I wonder..." I began.

"—how you can graciously decline the gift?" Ellie finished. I nodded. She rolled the top of the bag up and removed it from in front of me. "Leave it to me. I'll think of something."

"You save my life every single day," I said.

"Just remember that when you're figuring out the Christmas bonuses," she said.

fourteen

"You did what?" Sarge asked, his hands on his aproned hips.

I rested my face on the counter. It was cool. It felt delicious. The way my head was tilted, I could see out the door of Millie's Diner. I could see Scout sitting quietly outside the door, ready to greet new customers. What a good girl.

Then suddenly Jack was kneeling and petting her. Her stubby tail clocked back and forth. I lifted my head off the counter as he entered. "Hey, Sarge," he called.

"Padre," Sarge said.

I sat up. Jack didn't say anything to me, but he walked straight up to me, leaned in, and gave me a peck on the lips. It was completely unexpected, and it was nice.

"Look at you two," Sarge grinned. "Looks like this here thing you got going is...well, going."

"I hope so," Jack said, taking the stool next to mine. Once he was settled, I rested my head on his shoulder. "Tough day?" he asked me.

"Seems like those are the only kind there are right now," I said.

"That's because you care too much," he said.

"The priest says I care too much?" I asked.

"Yes, he does. You must take care of yourself, or you won't have anything to give anyone else. Self-care 101."

Sarge pointed at Jack. "That, right there."

I sniffed and straightened up. "What's the special, Sarge?"

"Lamb burger with goat cheese and spinach, topped with a balsamic reduction, on a brioche bun. Couscous with raisins and slivered almonds on the side."

"You had me at goat cheese," I said.

"Make that two," Jack said.

Sarge wrote up the order and passed it back to the kitchen. Then he poured me a glass of Merlot. Bless him.

"Father?" Sarge asked, holding up the bottle.

"I'll have one, too, thank you," Jack said.

Sarge poured another. Then he set the bottle back on the shelf behind him and wiped the counter with a dishrag. "So, Casey was just telling me about her little adventure."

I closed my eyes and shook my head slowly.

"Did she?" Jack asked.

"She did," Sarge said. "Good thing we serve criminals here."

"Ouch," I said.

"Hey, I been arrested a time or two," Sarge confessed. "How 'bout you, Father?"

"Sure. Protests."

"That's what I'm saying," Sarge said.

"Protests are another thing," I said. Neither of them argued. I sighed. "The worst part of it is, not only did I get caught, but it didn't even get me any closer to finding out who killed Betty Swann's dog."

"Why does it matter so much to you?" Sarge asked.

That stopped me. "I...that's a good question," I said. I tipped my head sideways, like Scout does when she doesn't understand something. "I guess it's because I love animals... especially dogs. And dog shows are...they have a lot of senti-mental...I have a lot of good memories there. If a dog isn't safe at a show, then..." I wasn't being very clear. Sarge and Jack were both nodding, however, so they seemed to be tracking with me. "I can only imagine how I would feel if something like that happened to Scout," I finished. "My heart goes out to Betty. I want to help her." I took a sip of the wine. "I feel like I let her down."

"Let's lay this out, like we do," Sarge said. "Who are your suspects?"

"Well, top of the pile are two women who own dogs that competed against Anselm. They posted threatening messages on Facebook—and they were there at the dog show."

"Motive and opportunity," Jack said.

"Exactly," I said. "If only I could have proven means."

"Who are these folks?" Sarge asked.

"One is Jessica Sneed," I said. "It was her house I...got caught in."

"I know Ms. Sneed. Has a German Shepherd named Andy," Sarge said.

I nodded.

"She shows me pictures whenever she's in. Comes for lunch on Fridays. Must be an old-time Catholic because she always orders the fish."

"Or she just likes fish," Jack said. "Could be a pescatarian."

"I seen one of them...what is it, a square thingy around her neck—"

"A scapular?" Jack asked. "Okay, old-time Catholic it is."

"What's a scapular?" I asked.

"It's kind of a necklace—it's a devotional thing," Jack kind-of explained.

"She's a nice lady," Sarge said.

"Not on Facebook," I countered.

"Well, people do strange things online." Sarge moved his head back and forth. "But I'm a pretty good judge of character. I don't think she could'a killed a dog. Who's the other one?"

I took the paper Ellie had given me out of my pocket. "Luna Mars."

Jack sat upright suddenly.

"That's a celestial name if I ever heard one," Sarge said.

"What?" I asked Jack, noting his reaction.

"Uh...Luna is our junior warden at the parish."

"What the hell is a junior warden?" I asked.

"He's speaking Episcopalian," Sarge said. "Do you know they got their own dictionaries? They can't even keep their vocabulary straight among themselves—have to have special dictionaries."

"Uh...that is true," Jack confessed, his shoulders deflating a little. "So, if you looked up 'junior warden' in the Episcopal dictionary, it would tell you that it's like the second chair in a church board of directors. The senior warden would be the chair, the junior warden is like the backup."

"Got it. Are all Christians this weird, or just Episcopalians?" I asked.

"Anglicans got their own proprietary brand of weird," Sarge opined.

Jack did not deny it. "What I'm saying is that I know Luna pretty well. I don't think she could have done this, either, but... I have noted a mean streak in her now and then."

"Talkin' out of school, Padre," Sarge warned.

"You're right. I didn't say that."

"You could pay her a pastoral visit, though," Sarge suggested, filling Jack's glass.

Jack looked up at him, and then over to me. "Uh...I'm not sure that's ethical."

"You gotta visit her anyway, sometime," Sarge shrugged. "Why not sooner rather than later? You can tell her about being at the dog show, seeing that dog die, how horrible it was. Watch her. See what kind of vibes you get."

There was a faraway look in Jack's eyes. He was nodding. "That...would be okay...I guess."

"One of us getting into trouble is enough," I said, placing a hand on his arm. He didn't respond, but only stared into the distance.

"Here's what I don't understand," Sarge said, opening a saltshaker and topping it off from an industrial-sized jar. "Why weren't you able to get the tox report?"

"Ms. Swann was a mess when her dog died," I said, remembering the scene vividly. "So the handler...handled things. He sent Anselm to a vet he works with, apparently, and tried to save money by only ordering the gross post."

"I guess vets got their own dictionaries, too," Sarge said, scowling.

"Sorry. Gross post refers to the visual examination of the body."

"Ah. What you can see with the naked eye, not using tests —which are expensive," Sarge reasoned.

"Exactly."

Sarge screwed the lid back on the saltshaker. "So...I hear you assigning a motive for not ordering the tox report, but it sounds to me like an assumption."

"What do you mean?" I asked.

"Well, you're telling yourself a story to explain things. You know the handler—what's his name?"

"Austin Teal," I said.

"Jeezuz, you sure he's not an action-movie character?"

I laughed. "It's his real name, far as I know."

"Okay, the handler didn't order a tox report," Sarge continued. "And the story you're telling yourself is that he did it to save money. Do you have any evidence to back up that story?"

I blinked. "Uh...no."

"So maybe he didn't order a tox report for some other reason...maybe to hide something."

"He did have the body cremated before we could get any other tests done," I said, nodding.

"Are you pulling my leg?" Sarge asked.

"I wish I was," I said.

"Little girl, why are you looking at anyone else?"

fifteen

"Ajeet, how did Toenail Club go?" I asked.

I had just poked my head into the break room. Ajeet was seated at the table, staring into his cup of coffee. His turban was woven from variegated threads of blue and green, and it matched his aqua scrubs perfectly. He glanced up and, for the first time in my experience with him, his eyes were cold.

I gripped the doorframe and cocked my head. "Ajeet?"

"Did you use Toenail Club as cover to break into that woman's house?" he asked.

My brain raced. Do I come clean, do I deflect, do I try to explain it away? His eyes narrowed as I hesitated. I sighed and my shoulders deflated. "Yes," I admitted.

"I came here under the illusion that you were a respectable, ethical veterinarian, Dr. Gibbons," he said, his brows furrowing. "It is personally painful to discover that I was wrong. I am not sure I can work beside you in good conscience." He looked down at his coffee cup. "And you have used me. And I feel like a fool...for having trusted you."

"Oh, Ajeet," I said. I closed the door to the break room and sat across from him at the table. "I'm sorry. I screwed up, big time. I was trying to help someone, but..."

"But you ended up hurting a lot of people."

I reared back a bit. "Who do you mean?" I asked.

"I mean everyone who thought well of you," he said. And with that, he rose from the table, dashed the rest of his coffee into the sink, placed his empty cup on the counter and left the room.

"Oh boy," I said, slumping over the table and putting my head down on my arms. For several minutes, I just breathed. Then I looked at my watch—Snoopy's hands told me that my break, such as it was, was over. I groaned and rose and went out, passing to the rear of the front desk, and snatched the next folder from the holder on the wall.

Just then my phone vibrated. I paused and pulled it out of the pocket of my lab coat. It was a text from Betty Swann. "Lunch at La Pinta?"

It was always a toss-up whether I would actually be able to leave the clinic when I was scheduled to—you never knew when a dog hit by a car would be rushed in, after all. But it seemed worth the risk. "Sure," I texted back. "12:30 okay?"

"See you there," she responded. I put the phone back in my coat and turned the knob into Exam Room Three. A cat with an abscess was waiting there with her owner. I lanced the abscess absently, and all the while Ajeet's words were echoing in my head. *You hurt a lot of people. Everyone who thought well of you...* I was so distraught I almost lanced my own thumb by accident.

Leaving the room, I wrote up my notes, entered them into the computer, and returned the file to the front desk. *Snap out of it, Casey. You're at work.* I needed something to distract me, and feline boils were not doing it.

What was I focused on before Ajeet threw me off track? *Austin Teal*, the voice in my head answered. *Focus on that*, I instructed my brain. I had planned to make some calls, just to see what I could find. I went to pick up my next folder, but Stacy shook her head. "No-show," she said. "But feel free to catch up on some paperwork." She pointed to a stack. Inventory and equipment order approvals. I picked up the stack, but once out of Stacy's sight, I plunked it down on the counter and didn't look at it again. I pulled out my phone and looked up the number of the president of the Utah City German Shepherd Club, Sarah Tandy. No one was home, so I left a message. Then I dialed the number for the vice-president, Mellie Davis.

"Hello?" I heard a voice answer. It had the wavery character of someone in an advanced stage of Parkinson's.

"Ms. Davis? Hi, I'm Doctor Casey Gibbons. I work at the Gold Country Vet Clinic."

"Oh, yes. You're the one who broke into Jessica's house."

I closed my eyes and pinched the bridge of my nose. "That's me," I said.

"That was a very naughty thing to do, my dear," she said.

I suddenly felt like I was being scolded by my grandmother. "Uh...yeah, it was pretty stupid. I was trying to help...oh, never mind. I wonder if I can ask you a couple of questions?"

"If I talk to you, do you promise not to break into my house?" she asked.

"I promise never to break into anyone's house ever again," I offered.

"All right, then. Would you like a cookie?"

I blinked. "Um...I would love a cookie."

"I'll get you a plate," she said. I heard a thud as she put the receiver down and then some rattling of dishes. Finally, though, she picked the phone up again. "There now. Snicker-doodles. The house specialty."

"It's very kind of you," I said, my eyes moving back and forth, wondering at the surreality of it. It occurred to me that, however much Mellie Davis knew, she might not be the most reliable of narrators.

"Um...I assume you know Austin Teal," I said.

"Oh, yes. Very tall. He's a looker. I was thinking just the other day what it would be like to wiggle and giggle with that one."

I was tempted to say, "TMI," but instead I pressed ahead. "What can you tell me about him?"

"Oh, well, not much, dear. He's fairly new. I think he's only been handling around here for a year...maybe a little more."

I wondered about Ms. Davis' sense of time and made a mental note to verify this elsewhere. "How many of your members' dogs does he handle?"

"Oh, two or three. There was Anselm...so sad about Anselm."

"Yes," I agreed.

"And then there's Braunschweiger, Dolores Black's dog."

I wrote that down. "Do you have some contact information on Ms. Black?"

"If I give it to you, do you promise not to break into her house?"

I rolled my eyes. "I promise."

"All right. Just a moment..." I heard a clunk as she dropped the receiver. After what seemed like an eternity, she picked it up again. "Had to find my little black book."

"Did you find it?"

"Yes, of course, dear. Don't be impertinent."

I frowned.

"Here it is. Marjory Seacrest—"

"No, Ms. Davis. You were looking up Dolores Black."

"Oh, yes, so I was." I heard the tinny sound of pages being turned. "Here it is. Silly of me."

She gave me the number and I jotted it down.

"I'm not giving you the address," she warned.

"That's just fine," I said. "Thank you so much."

"You're very rude, you know."

I jerked upright. "What? How have I been rude?"

"You didn't even touch your cookie."

sixteen

I rushed into the La Pinta Mexican Restaurant at 12:35 exactly. Five minutes late seemed like on-time to me, at least on-time enough. But I didn't see Betty Swann. I wondered if she could have left in a huff because I wasn't there at 12:30 on the dot. No, I decided, that didn't seem likely. What was most likely was that she was simply running late herself.

A hostess seated me and I let her know that we'd need two menus. She installed me in a booth where I could easily see the door. She returned quickly with two glasses of ice water, then spun away with a smile.

I glanced at the menu, but I didn't really see it. I loved Mexican food, but it did not, in general, like me very much. It was a sure-fire invitation to heartburn. But was it worth it? I contemplated the enchiladas and realized that if I had two of those, along with beans and rice, I'd pitch forward into carb-loaded narcolepsy before I saw my next client. It would be the salad, I decided, the protests of my enchilada-loving inner child notwithstanding.

I put the menu back down on the table and took a sip of the

ice water. It smelled vaguely of chlorine, which I chose to ignore. I glanced at my watch. Snoopy, in the midst of his happy dance, informed me that it was 12:45. Still no Betty Swann.

I pursed my lips and crossed my arms. I hated being stood up. And it wasn't like Betty would have forgotten—I'd gotten her text only two hours ago. Besides, it was she who had requested the meeting.

I wondered if perhaps she had heard about my arrest in the interim and had decided that breaking tortillas with a criminal was beneath her. *Don't be ridiculous,* the voice in my head warned. *That's your shame talking.*

I did have a good deal of shame about the incident, it was true. What had I been thinking? And now I was doing everything I could to *avoid* thinking about it. It was simply too painful.

And scary.

And why did I need the extra drama in my life right now? Why was I doing this? Wasn't life exciting enough with my work, my relationship with Jack? If I needed a hobby, what was wrong with origami, for heaven's sake?

I pinched the skin of my thenar space and the momentary pain brought me back to the moment. I looked at Snoopy again. 12:50.

A couple of minutes later, the waitress stopped by and asked if I was ready. *I do need to eat, Betty or no Betty,* I thought. I ordered the salad.

I wondered if perhaps something had happened to her. I felt for my phone and considered calling Gus. No, I decided. That would be an abuse of his infatuation.

I ate my boring salad absently, chewing the cud of the events of the past several days with more attention than I was giving to the lettuce. I fantasized about swinging by St.

Julian's-in-the-Valley to surprise Jack and maybe steal a kiss before returning to work. I wouldn't do it, but I loved the fantasy. There was something about seeing him in his dog collar that revved my engines, although I'd never admit that to him. No doubt the transgression of kissing a priest, planted deep in the brain of this recovering Catholic girl, had something to do with it. I wondered what it would be like to make love to that priest. Jack had asked me to go away for the weekend. Did he hope that might include carnal intimacy? I secretly hoped it would.

Somehow, without my realizing it, my salad was gone. I paid the check and left the restaurant, more than a little bit worried about Betty. Before I got into my car, I texted her. "So sorry I missed you. Are you alright?"

I put the phone back in my pocket and opened the car door. Then my phone rang. I pulled it out and was relieved to see Betty's name on the screen. I accepted the call and put the phone to my ear. "Betty, I'm so glad to hear from you."

But it wasn't Betty's voice I heard. It was Gus. "Casey?" he asked.

"Gus? What the hell? Why are you answering Betty's phone?"

"Because Betty can't."

"So how do you have her phone?"

"Casey, Betty is...I'm sorry to have to tell you like this, but... there's been an accident. Ms. Swann is dead."

seventeen

The forest was ablaze with red and blue flashing lights. I parked a respectful distance away, and then joined a small gaggle of local folks watching as firefighters and rescue crews tended to the smashed vintage Cadillac.

"Off the road!" a deputy I didn't know was shouting, and the gaggle shuffled toward the shoulder. I am not tall, and I struggled to see above the shoulders in front of me. *Propriety be damned*, I thought, and pushed through to the front. Police tape strung from cones pressed against my waist while the tiny mass of the curious jostled at my back. But I could see.

At once, I wished I couldn't. There are things you see accidentally, things that you never want to see, things you can never unsee. It was one of those.

I could see the black scorch marks of tires on the road. Betty Swann's Cadillac had not made the tight turn in the road, but had plunged off the embankment. Now its tattered, dented carcass was cradled in the forked branches of a large tree, hovering about twelve feet above the ground. Through the open driver's-side door I could see the body of Betty Swann dangling in free air, bent back at an impossible angle, her leg caught in the tangled wreckage. Her dress had fallen down over her face, revealing her indignity to the world. It was horrible.

I forced myself to look away, even as those around me snapped pictures on their phones. I wanted to yell at them, to shame them into allowing her some privacy, but I knew it would have done little good. I forced my eyes away from Betty's hanging body and focused on the rescue attempt.

That's when I saw Gus coming toward me. His face wasn't angry, exactly, but it was not happy. "All right, back, everybody. Don't press against the tape. It's there for your safety and for the integrity of the accident scene." He was addressing everyone, but he walked directly up to me. He lowered his eyes to meet mine and what seemed like a long moment of silence passed as he searched for my soul. I'm not sure he found it, but he said, "You just had to see it for yourself, didn't you?"

"Of course I did. This isn't an accident, Gus. It can't be."

"That seems to be your default mode," he said.

"I wasn't wrong about Shelley," I said, referring to my murdered partner at the clinic—and my friend. The Sheriff's Office had written her death off as an accident, but I knew in my gut there was foul play—and I proved it. "And I'm not wrong about this."

I met his eyes again and did not see incredulity. That was reassuring. He didn't think it was an accident either. He just couldn't say so...yet. That was all right. He was a professional, and I respected his reticence.

He turned, but I leaned over the tape and caught his elbow. He turned back. "Gus, she has a dog—"

"I thought her dog died," he frowned.

"Her dog Anselm was murdered, but she has another dog. Can you send someone to her house? But please don't send animal control. I'll board her dog until we can locate the next-of-kin."

"I'll take that under advisement," he said.

"Don't be an ass, Gus," I said. "I don't want that dog to suffer."

He looked angry for a moment, but then softened. "I'll check it out, Case. I promise."

That was good enough. I watched as he walked back to the scene. Despite all that was going on, I could not help but think that he had a cute butt. I hated myself for that. I forced myself to focus. There was no way to get closer to the accident. Besides, I wasn't sure I wanted to see any more of it than I already had.

I disentangled myself from the growing crowd and made my way back to my car. There was a long line of cars parked on the shoulder now as more and more people stopped to gawk. And the road was closed, so it was either that or turn back and go the way they came.

I got into the car, phoned the clinic, and punched in Ellie's extension. I waited for the Bluetooth on my stereo to pick up the call, then made a U-turn to head back to the clinic.

Ellie picked up on the third ring. "Hey, boss," she said.

"Hey. I have bad news. Betty Swann just died in a car accident."

"Oh my God!" Ellie breathed. "I knew about the accident—it's coming up on my news feed. But they haven't released the name of the deceased yet. Are you sure?"

"I'm sure. Gus told me."

"Can't he get in trouble for that?"

"He didn't do it on purpose. I called Betty—we were supposed to have lunch—and Gus just happened to be holding her cell phone at the time."

"Jeez," Ellie said. "I'm so, so sorry."

"So am I. It was...horrible."

"How can I help?"

"I need to find out who Betty's next-of-kin is."

"Okay, I'm on it. But...shouldn't the police break that news?"

"I'm not going to jump the gun on them. I just...I want to make sure Betty's other dog is okay."

"Ah...you want to shepherd the adoption."

"Something like that," I said. "We have no idea who will be held responsible for Betty's other dog—"

"Abelard," Ellie reminded me. "Her other dog's name is Abelard."

"That's right. How did you know—?"

"There are pictures on her Facebook page."

"Of course there are. Can you pull a couple of those pictures for me?"

"Absolutely. Want me to email or text them to you?"

"Either way."

"On it," she said.

"Thanks, El. See you in five." I hung up and concentrated on the road. Someone had killed Anselm. And now someone had killed his owner. And I was willing to bet it was the same someone.

eighteen

As soon as I got off work, I texted Gus. "Did you find Abelard?"

He didn't immediately answer, so I drove home. I don't think I noticed a single second of that journey. All I could see was Betty Swann swinging upside down from the suspended wreckage of her car.

As I entered the door to my cottage, Scout bounced in her joy. The incongruence between how she was feeling and how I was feeling was profound. It occurred to me that it would do me no harm to absorb a little bit of her giddiness, but it was easier said than done.

Instead, I sat cross-legged on the floor and tried to hug her. It was like trying to hug a tornado. Finally, though, she settled down enough for me to put my head against her chest and just feel her vital warmth. She felt strong and wholesome and deeply good. And I needed that feeling. I pressed my nose into her fur and inhaled. It smelled like comfort.

When I pulled back, her eyes were fixed on my face, and she was wagging. "Let's work. What do you say?"

As I reached for the nylon treat bag, she began bouncing again. *Tigger has nothing on Scout*, I thought. We went out to the front yard and went through our obedience routine. We did Eyes on Me, Heel, Sit-Stay, Down-Stay, Stay-and-Fetch. Then we worked on the item that was our growing edge—Play Dead.

"Okay, girl. Ready?" I held up a treat so she could see it. "Play dead."

As if a puppeteer had let go of the strings, Scout collapsed to the ground. I was worried that she'd hit her head, but she was too smart for that. She lay spread-eagled, nipples-up, remaining absolutely motionless.

Motionless, that is, except for one eye fixed directly on me. "No, Scout." I moved my hand over her eyes, gently pushing her lid down. Amazingly, it stuck, and I counted five seconds of absolute, perfect play-deadness.

"Okay! Good girl!" I shouted. Scout leaped up and snarfled the treat from my fingers.

We tried it a couple more times, but each time she kept one eye open, until I "fixed" it. I sighed. Maybe tomorrow she'd do better. I wondered if perhaps I ought to withhold the treat the next time she did it wrong. The problem was, I was such a softy —something Scout exploited shamelessly.

Once back inside, I filled her bowl with kibble, added a spoonful of wet food for spice, and set her puzzle bowl on the floor. She attacked it with gusto, finishing it off before I could pour myself a whisky.

I knocked back the scotch and closed my eyes, feeling the warm tendrils of the liquor seep into my muscles and relax them. "That is...much, much better," I said aloud to no one in particular.

My phone vibrated and I fished it out of my pocket. The screen said "GUS." I touched the green button. "Hey, Gus."

"Hey, Case."

"Did you find Abelard?"

"Nope."

"No?"

"I'm here at the house now. There's no dog here."

"There are sometimes kennels in the garage or an outbuilding—"

"I already checked. I can see where the kennels are. There's no dog in them."

"Okay. Thanks, Gus." I hung up and chewed on my lip. Scout was sniffing at a clump of weeds near the mailbox. She was a little too close to the road for my comfort, so I called her back. She bounded toward me and we went into the house. Time for *my* dinner, I thought.

My phone buzzed again, and I looked down. This time it was a text from Ellie. Opening it, I discovered it was an address. "What's this?" I typed.

"Betty Swann NOK," she wrote.

It only took me a moment to figure out the acronym: Betty Swann's next-of-kin.

nineteen

The next day was, blessedly, my day off. I picked Jack and Tripod up on my way out of town, and Jack gave Scout a good nuzzle before settling in and buckling his seat belt. I was relieved to see that he was not wearing his clerical collar. "Where are we going?" he asked.

"We're going to see Betty Swann's next-of-kin," I answered.

"I know that," he said. "What I want to know is where she lives, or where are we meeting her? How far are we going?"

"Oh. Sorry. Davis. She lives in Davis."

"That's not so bad," he said.

"Do you have appointments this afternoon?" I asked.

"I have some hospital visits to make, so my time is pretty flexible today. If we get back by one or two o'clock, I'll be fine."

"Don't you have a sermon to work on or something?" I asked, making a left onto Utah City's Main Street.

"I have the weekend off, remember?" Jack asked.

Ouch, I thought. Yes, I remembered. He'd asked me to go

away with him, and I'd blown him off. To break the awkward-ness, I asked, "What was your sermon about last week?"

He cocked his head. "You really want to know?"

"Sure," I said, hoping I sounded convincing.

"Jeremiah smashes the jar in front of the leaders of Judah. 'Doom! Doom!' he cries, and says, 'I the Lord will smash you just like I smashed this pot!'"

"Cheery," I grimaced.

"Political street theater," Jack smiled.

"Is that what that is?" I asked.

"Full on."

"Wasn't that written, like, almost in caveman days?" I asked. "How can you take it seriously?"

"Uh...it's a bit removed from caveman days, although it is ancient," Jack admitted. "But people don't change—the problems and dilemmas they wrote about are all still with us. I read scripture to learn from our ancestors, but I also get to talk back to them."

"Is that what you do in your sermons?" I asked.

"Oh, absolutely. It's not a monologue, it's a debate. I call reading scripture 'arguing with Grandpa.'"

I laughed out loud. "You are so freaking weird."

"That's what you love about me—" Jack started, but then caught himself. He shifted uneasily. "Uh...that's what you *like* about me. Sorry. That was awkward."

I kept my eyes on the road and swallowed. "It's okay," I said. "Moving slow."

"Moving slow," he agreed.

The following silence was awkward, so I passed him my phone and said, "Indigo girls."

He held the camera up to my face to satisfy security, and once in I saw his thumbs flashing over the screen. "Any partic-ular album?" he asked.

"Surprise me," I said.

He lit on *Nomads, Indians, Saints*, and as soon as the first rocking notes of "Hammer and a Nail" rang out, he relaxed into his seat. I was surprised—and impressed—that he not only knew all of the lyrics, but he was also singing the harmony parts.

"I didn't know you were an Amy and Emily fan," I said.

"You see? We have so much to discover about each other," he said, raising his voice over the music.

"Huh."

"They're one of the most theologically literate groups making music today," he said. "Emily's father is a world-famous theologian. Methodist."

"Oh, really?" I wasn't sure why that surprised me, but it did. "How famous can he be if I didn't know that?"

"How many theologians can you name?" he asked.

"Uh...none," I admitted.

"Famous is relative. Don Saliers. Among church geeks, he's well-known, at least in his area."

"Area?"

"Area of theology."

"There are areas of theology?" I asked. He lowered his head and narrowed one eye at me. "I'll take your word for that, then," I grinned. Fortunately, he grinned back.

For most of the rest of the way there, we simply listened to the girls, and I let myself be serenaded by Jack as he sang along. What amazed me was that he seemed to feel no embarrassment to be singing so loudly for so long. I was a little embarrassed for him, but a voice in my head reminded me that was my problem, not his.

After a little more than an hour, my GPS guided us to a two-story apartment building the color of Pepto-Bismal.

"Does she know we're coming?" Jack asked, as he got out of the car.

I shut my own door. "Yes. I spoke to her briefly this morning."

"Anything to know?"

I shrugged. "She seemed nice enough."

I double-checked to make sure the windows were cracked and the dogs would be okay. It was still early in the day and cool. The sky was overcast, so I didn't worry about their getting overheated. But I reminded myself to keep an eye on the sun, just in case.

We climbed a rickety staircase that looked like it might be rotted through. Close up, I could see the cracked paint and crumbling corners of the apartment building. Bits of chicken wire stuck out from the damaged adobe in numerous places.

I found the door to the apartment and knocked. I heard a rumbling in the house, and a moment later, the door swung suddenly inward. "Howdy!"

I involuntarily took a step back at the forcefulness of the greeting. Or perhaps it was the wildness of the woman who greeted us. She was large, in a printed muumuu festooned with bright pictures of toucans. Her yellow hair hung in dreadlocks, and bits of yarn in wildly diverse colors were woven into the dreads. She had on way too much mascara, but otherwise wore no makeup. I could also smell her body odor from where I stood nearly four feet away.

"You must be the doctor," she said.

I put out my hand. "I'm Doctor Casey Gibbons."

"And who's this handsome fella?" She pointed at Jack.

"Uh...he's my friend. He's just along for the ride. His name is Jack."

"Nice lips," she said. Jack said nothing, but his eyebrows

rose dramatically. "You kissed those lips of his?" she asked me directly.

"Uh...I'm here to talk about your sister," I said. "Can we come in?"

"Oh, how silly of me. Please come in." She swung the door wide, and we both entered.

I was instantly sorry. The reek of BO was even more profound in the house, but other smells were even stronger. These were odors I knew well—soiled litterbox and cat piss.

My nose did not deceive me. I'm not sure how many cats lived in that small apartment, but at first glance I counted more than twenty. But what was odder than the number of cats were the cats themselves. Every one of them was wearing a shiny silver vest, made of what looked like mylar, or whatever space blankets are made of. They looked well made, and the cats did not seem to mind them, but... I looked at Jack. I could tell he was struggling to maintain a neutral affect.

"You have...uh...a lot of cats," Jack said.

"Oh, you have to have cats if you want to stay safe from the Millidor Empire. The problem is—" she pointed at Jack and narrowed one eye. "Protecting the *cats*."

"Thus, the vests," Jack said.

"Exactly," the woman nodded. Then a change came over her, and she seemed to momentarily forget where she was or what she was doing. She reached for the back of a chair and steadied herself. Then reason came back into her eyes and she chuckled a bit. "I'm so sorry," she said, affecting a breezy demeanor. "What a rude host. I'm Bree Swann. Please have a seat." She indicated a loveseat. It was hard to tell its original color as it was covered in what looked like decades of cat hair. I steeled myself and sat on it. Jack did the same. *Clothes wash*, the voice in my head reminded me.

Jack reached over and squeezed my hand. He met my eye

and nodded. It was encouragement. I wasn't sure I needed it, but I was grateful for it. He let go of my hand and sat back.

Bree Swann sat in the chair that had been her support. "Shall I get us some tea?"

Not wanting to face a fresh horror, I held my hand up. "No, please. We're fine."

"Very well. But you let me know. I have some soft cheeses in the fridge. They're not too moldy yet."

I forced my face to keep still as I imagined a plate full of soft cheese with tufts of cat hair sticking out of it at all angles. "No, thank you. We're not hungry."

"I'm taking Casey out for lunch," Jack said, leaning in conspiratorially. "It's a special lunch, and we don't want to spoil our appetites."

"Oh. Of course. We wouldn't want that."

She looked eager to hear more, but I changed the subject. "Ms. Swann, I'm so, so sorry about Betty. You must be devastated."

Bree looked confused for a moment. Then she looked over at the window and her face fell. "Oh yes. Now I remember. Betty. She was a bitch on wheels, that one."

I blinked. "Oh?"

"Sooner spite you than look at you." She looked ready to spit.

"Well...I'm sorry to hear that."

"She was mother's favorite. She got the education, you know. I didn't. And when mama died, she got the money." She sighed. "Thank the rebel powers for SSI."

I felt taken aback. "I'm sorry. I was under the impression that you were...that everything Betty had..."

Bree cocked her head. "Oh. You mean the will?"

"Yes."

"Oh, yes. She left everything to charity." She smiled sadly. "Not to me."

"I'm sorry to hear that," I said. My shoulders sagged.

"Everything except her dog."

I perked up again. "Well, thank God for that."

"Oh, yes?"

"Yes...I mean...that's why we've come. You see, we believe that Anselm—your sister's other dog—was murdered. And I think your sister was, too. And I think the two were probably linked."

I could see her eyes moving back and forth but had no idea if any connections were being made. "I'll get some tea," she said, getting up and heading into what must have been the kitchen.

I hung my head and moaned.

"Do you want some soft cheeses?" she called from the other room.

"No, thank you," Jack called back. He leaned into me and whispered. "Hang in there. You're making headway."

"Am I? I feel so sorry for her."

"So do I." He reached for my hand again. This time I squeezed back. Then I picked a tuft of cat hair off of Jack's sweater and let it fall lazily to the floor. "We're going to need to shear each other when this is over."

Jack gave me a sly grin. "If that's a euphemism, it sounds like fun."

"You are a very naughty priest."

Eventually, Bree came out of the kitchen with a tray containing three mugs and a teapot, complete with knitted cozy. The cozy, too, was covered in matted hair.

She sat the tray down on an ottoman and shooed two of the curious, silver-vested cats away from it. She poured tea into the cups and lifted the lid off a sugar bowl. Even from the distance I sat I could see dead bugs mixed in with the sugar—at least, I hoped they were dead.

"I take mine black," I said.

"Me too, thank you," Jack offered, a bit too quickly.

"Suit yourselves," she said, spooning four teaspoons of sugar into her own cup. She handed our cups to us, and while I received it, I could neither bring myself to look at it nor drink from it.

"Ms. Swann—" I began.

"Please call me Bree," she interrupted.

"All right, then. Bree, I am afraid for your sister's other dog, Abelard."

"He's a handsome boy." For a moment, she looked proud.

"He is. I've seen pictures," I said. I waited until I caught her eye, then held it. "Bree, I'm afraid for him."

"Afraid? Whyever for?"

"Because I think that whoever killed your sister and Anselm might want him dead, too."

"But why?"

I sat back a bit. "I don't know that."

"But you suspect he is in danger?"

"I do."

She stared at her cup and frowned. "I don't want to see him..."

"Hurt?" I suggested. "Or worse?"

She looked up at me and nodded. "I don't want that. No matter what a saucy cow my sister was."

"Do you know where he is now? Abelard?"

"Oh, yes. He's with that handsome handler, what's his name...?"

"Austin Teal?" I offered.

She snapped her fingers. "That's him!"

"Have you met him?"

"No…but I see my sister's Facebook posts."

"Ah."

"Have you been in touch with Mr. Teal?"

"Yes. He phoned a couple days ago—just after…you know."

"Yes. After Betty died."

She looked at her naked toes, stained and curled like potato chips. She nodded.

"You didn't like your sister," Jack said, "but you still loved her."

Bree looked up at Jack and nodded.

"I understand that. I have an older brother…he was always very mean to me when we were growing up. He still is."

I didn't know that. What else didn't I know about Jack? Probably a lot. That worried me, but I couldn't let it distract me. "Bree, can I ask what you and Mr. Teal talked about?"

"Well, yes. Since Abelard is now mine, he wanted to make sure I wanted him to continue to be shown. He told me that, in the show world, getting a championship is the only way for a dog to be protected. I think he said Abelard has…oh, what was it?"

"Abelard has twelve of fifteen needed points, and one of two needed majors," I said.

"That's it!" Bree pointed at me.

"How on earth did you know that?" Jack asked.

"Give me some credit. I know how to use the interwebs," I said. Teal was absolutely right about how to protect a dog, and I had looked up Abelard's stats on his breeder's site just before we left. I turned back to Bree. "So, did you agree to allow Teal to continue showing Abelard?"

"Well, I wasn't sure at first," Bree said, twirling one of her dreadlocks. Then she put it in her mouth and sucked on the end of it. I remember sucking on a blanket when I was a child. It tasted sour every time I put it in my mouth. I imagined that dreadlock must have tasted the same way. She removed it and said, "It's so expensive."

"Yes, well that's true." I looked around at the shabby apartment. Bree Swann might be a secret billionaire eccentric enough to live in Section 8 housing, but I wasn't betting on it. "So what did you decide?"

"He said he would see Abelard through to his championship for free...and that he'd keep showing him, even after that. No cost! I don't know what I'd do with a dog here, so of course I said yes."

My mind raced. Why on earth would a professional handler like Teal agree to show a dog for free? Out of the goodness of his heart, perhaps? I wasn't buying it. He had simply seemed too slimy.

"Besides, I'd have to make him a mylar jacket to protect him from alien influences. It would have to be big. Do you know how expensive mylar is? I have to eat the cat's food for a week every time I have to make one for my boobookins here." She indicated a random cat.

I didn't know what Teal was up to, but my alarm bells were ringing. And my intuition was rarely wrong. I needed to see for myself. The problem was, I had no authority to say what happened to the dog. The only one who did was Bree Swann. "Bree, where is Abelard's next show?"

"San Diego, dear. This weekend."

I weighed our options. I was off this weekend, and I knew Jack was off—he'd asked me to go away with him, after all. "Uh...Bree...why don't we go see Abelard in action?"

"What? In San Diego?"

"Sure. Why not?"

Out of the corner of my eye, I saw Jack's eyebrows lift nearly off his head. "Uh..." he started, but I plowed ahead.

"Sure. We'll all drive down together. You'll get a good sense of your new dog, and we'll get to see Mr. Teal in action...and get a feel for...well, for whether he really has Abelard's best interests in mind."

"But I can't leave my cats," Bree complained.

"Sure you can. Just leave out some food and water and clean their litter boxes. They'll be fine for 48 hours. They're cats."

"But without someone to perform the rituals, how will I keep them safe from the Millidor Empire?"

"Oh, yes. The Millidor Empire," I said.

Just then, one of Bree's cats lurched unsteadily and fell over. I leaped out of the couch and knelt by the prostrate feline. I touched its head. "It's too hot," I said.

"Oh, never mind him. I just put them in the refrigerator for a few minutes whenever that happens. They're right as rain after that." Unceremoniously, she lifted the cat and trotted off to the kitchen. I heard the refrigerator door slam, and Bree walked back in.

"Bree, I'm a veterinarian," I said.

"Yes? I think I knew that. Did I know that? Yes, I did." Bree smiled.

"Those vests are very warm, and it is already, what, 75 degrees in here?"

"At least," Jack said. I suddenly noticed how uncomfortable he looked in his sweater. I imagined he didn't want to take it off, lest he get cat hair all over his shirt, too.

"I think your cats are overheating from the mylar...sheaths they're trapped in."

"But if I don't protect them from the—"

"Yes, the Millidor Empire," I said, chewing my lip. "Wait, I thought they were keeping you safe from the...the Millidor Empire—"

"It's a reciprocal relationship," she snapped, as if that should be obvious.

"Uh...okay," I said, "What is the Millidor Empire doing to them?"

"Why, it wants to use them to influence the masses."

"The masses?" Jack asked.

"Not your kind of masses," I said.

"I know that," Jack said. "Bree, how would your cats influence a lot of people?"

"With the FaceBook. And the Tweeter."

"Your cats use the computer?" I asked.

"I can't watch them every minute," she confessed. "They're very, very sneaky. And if their minds are being controlled from..." she pointed to the ceiling. It was yellowed and cracked and the remains of a long spiderweb hung down into the middle of the room.

"Ah, I think I see," Jack said. "The transmissions from the Millidor Empire must be interrupted, so that your cats cannot wreak havoc on humanity."

"Yes," Bree's eyes widened. "That's it exactly."

"You are a very brave, very clever woman," Jack said.

"I do what I can." Bree looked very satisfied with herself.

"I think I have another solution," Jack said.

"Oh, yes?"

"Yes. Have you ever studied feng shui?"

"No, but I have heard of it," Bree confessed. So had I, but I had no idea where Jack was going with this.

"It's all about controlling the flow of energy in a room...or a house...or an apartment." He smiled patiently.

"Tell me more," Bree's face lit up with wonder.

"If you put a mylar hexagon—you know, a shape with six equal sides—in every corner of the room, you can effect the same protection as the vests now afford. They wouldn't have to be very large—you can probably repurpose one of the vests. With all the vests you've got here, you could do every corner in your whole apartment." Jack leaned in conspiratorially, putting his wrists on his knees, clasping his hands. "And the thing is, with hexagons, you can charge them before you go. You can use the same rituals—those will work just fine, but you can double up on them. The hexagons will hold the ritual energy for several days if you charge them up before you go."

Bree's eyes were wide. "Are you making fun of me?"

Jack's hand went to his chest. "Far from it. I am an Episcopal priest. I know a thing or two about ritual energies."

"Like Bishop Leadbeater in the *Science of the Sacraments*!" she said, her eyes widening.

"Yes, exactly so," Jack said. "Are you a Theosophist?"

"Oh yes. I am in constant contact with the Ascended Masters."

"Please give my humble regards to Koot Hoomi, won't you?" Jack said.

"Oh! Mr.—I don't remember your name—"

"You can call me Father Mornington," Jack said.

"Oh, Father. You do understand!"

"Very well. And if you like, I can bless your apartment before we leave, just to make sure that we have a bubble of angelic protection as well."

"Oh! That does sound lovely. You know I haven't been outside for..." she looked away. "Eighteen years? No, nineteen."

"Well, it's about time. The sun will feel good on your skin," Jack said.

"Yes, I suppose it will." She looked around, flustered. "I have a lot of work to do. Where is my sewing basket?"

"Thank you for your time, Ms. Swann," I said. "We'll pick you up early on Friday morning. Will that be all right? Say, 8:00am?"

"Oh, that will be fine, dear." But she wasn't really paying attention to me. She had already stripped one of the vests off of the nearest cat and was ripping out the seams. The cat looked relieved.

"We can find the way out," Jack said. "The Lord bless you and keep you."

"Thank you, dear. And may the Master Jesus reveal the World Teacher soon."

Jack gestured toward the door. I didn't object. "Bree, don't forget the cat in the fridge!" I called over my shoulder.

Once outside, we closed the door and took a deep breath. Jack instantly took off his sweater. I could see beads of sweat dripping down his neck.

"That was...weird," I said.

He shrugged. "Eh. Theosophy."

"Do I even want to know what that is?"

"I'll tell you all about it on the ride home," he said.

"I can't wait." I unlocked the car and got in.

Before I could start the engine, however, Jack asked, "So...I guess we're going away for the weekend after all?"

My shoulders fell. "Yeah. I'm...I'm sorry about that. I know it's not the romantic getaway you were hoping for."

"I'm not really letting myself hope too much," he said.

I don't know why, but that stung. "What do you mean?" I asked.

"Well...you're a little stand-offish. I don't want to hope for...I don't want to be disappointed."

"Are you going to get serious about me?" I asked.

He smiled, but it was a sad smile. "I already am."

twenty

When we pulled up to Bree Swann's apartment building on Friday, we were surprised to see her outside waiting for us. Beside her was an old-fashioned carpetbag adorned with a paisley print. Bree was wearing a different muumuu, this one sporting stripes in all the colors of the rainbow.

Jack jumped out and grabbed her carpetbag, which he stowed in the back of Old Blue, my pumpkin-colored Honda Civic. Bree squeezed into the back seat and immediately reclined, spreading out to fill the available space.

Jack resumed his place in the passenger seat and closed the door. "What about the angelic blessing?" Bree asked.

"Right!" Jack said. He leaped from the car and faced North. He closed his eyes and passed the edge of his upright hand down his face, forehead to nose to chin. Then he stretched it out, holding his index and middle fingers up, as if they were stuck together. Eyes closed, his mouth moved inaudibly. Then he turned to the East and did exactly the same thing. Then again to the South and then to the West.

He jumped back into the car and flashed Bree a smile over his shoulder. "Michael, Gabriel, Raphael, and Uriel are *on it.*"

"Thank you," Bree said, apparently satisfied with that eccentric performance.

Jack closed the car door, then looked over at me and our eyes met. His widened as he began to detect what I was already painfully aware of. The odor emanating from the back seat was so powerful as to be almost intoxicating—and not in a good way. With almost synchronized movements, we both cracked our windows.

We backtracked to Sacramento to pick up Highway 5 and settled in for the long, boring drive south.

"I feel bad leaving the dogs behind," Jack said. "I mean, it's a dog show. They would have had such a good time."

"They would," I agreed. "But where would we have put them?"

"Mitt Romney would let them ride on the roof," Jack said.

"Ha!" I laughed out loud. "They'll be fine at the clinic. Besides, they get to stay together in the same run."

"They do seem to get along well," Jack said.

I opened my mouth to say, *It bodes well for a future pack*, but realized how forward that was. *Moving slow*, I reminded myself.

I had been a little freaked out when Jack confessed that he was getting serious about me. Was I getting serious about him? I wasn't sure. After Dennis and I split up, I had kind of written off the idea of ever getting serious about anyone again. It wasn't as if I didn't want to have a partner...someday. I just wasn't eager to get tangled up in another emotional mess...or another divorce. And frankly, as a vet, who has time? I hadn't been looking for a boyfriend, much less a partner. And yet, here was Jack. He wasn't perfect, but neither was I. I knew I didn't need perfect, but I think I did need *perfect for me*. And the jury was still out on that one. Jack had a lot going for him. He was smart, he was kind. He was game for almost anything. He loved animals. But he was also profoundly religious. It grated at me, and I didn't really know why.

Suddenly, our passenger began belting out Janis Joplin's "Me and Bobby McGee." To my amusement, Jack joined in after the first verse. And despite myself, all three of us were singing by the end of the song.

"Bathroom break," Bree said.

We had been on the road for more than two hours, so that seemed fair. We'd just passed the exit for Patterson, and I pulled off at the next ramp. I topped off the tank at the Mobile station, and after we had all freshened up and bought snacks and drinks, we headed for the highway again.

The next hour was spent with Jack and Bree discussing whether some fellow named Krishnamurti had really been the World Teacher or not. Jack opined that Bishop Leadbeater—whoever that is—had been mistaken about Krishnamurti. Bree countered that the good bishop was infallible, and that "dark powers" had derailed Krishnamurti from his intended destiny. It was a fascinating discussion, even though I had no idea who any of these people were or why they mattered. They seemed to matter to Bree and Jack, so I imagined they must be a big deal to someone. What amazed me most, however, was how conversant Jack seemed to be in the subject. Was there anything even tangentially connected to religion that he didn't know? If there was, I hadn't found it yet.

The conversation had just taken a turn into deconstructing Krishnamurti's freestyle antinomianism—whatever that meant—and my attention was starting to drift when my phone rang.

I punched the flashing button on my console and waited for Bluetooth to do its connecting thing. "Hello?" I asked.

For the first time in an hour, Jack and Bree fell silent. At first I thought it was a sales call that didn't connect, but then a weak voice was barely audible over the rush of the road. I turned up the volume on my stereo. "Is this Casey Gibbons?"

"Yes, this is she," I said. I pushed down my left turn indicator and passed a semi.

"This is Sarah Tandy. You left a message for me a few days ago. About Austin Teal."

I jerked upright, my attention once again sharply focused. "Yes, Ms. Tandy. Thank you so much for returning my call."

"You wanted to know about my experience with Mr. Teal. Are you thinking of using him to handle your dog?"

"Something like that," I lied. Jack shook his head. "What has your experience with him been like?" I asked.

"Uh...mixed. On the plus side, he is an able handler, and he took our Water Dog Boone all the way to champion."

"And on the minus side?" I asked.

"Well, it was weird," she said. "He told us he'd be back with Boone—back from the show—oh, I forget the date. But anyway, we—my husband and I—went to his house to pick Boone up. But when we got there, Mr. Teal seemed nervous. We asked to see Boone, but instead of letting us, he insisted that we go out to celebrate his championship. It was ten in the morning, so that was a little weird. But he was insistent and brought us to this very cute bakery. We'd already had breakfast, and it was too early for lunch, so we got coffees and a Danish and tried to make the best of it."

"How long did he keep you out?" I asked.

"Well, that was the weird thing. It was hours. He kept ordering more and more, even after we very clearly told him we didn't want any. He insisted we walk around downtown and visit the shops. Finally, my husband got angry—I can hardly blame him. I was ready to scream."

"And what happened then?" I asked.

"He looked at his watch and agreed. Kept checking his phone, too. But he really took his time. He even got lost once—and he lives there! Finally, however, we got back to the house. He went and got Boone, and he was just as pleasant and relaxed as ever after that. I didn't understand it at all. And...I don't mind saying, I just don't trust him now. You don't happen to know of another handler that you trust, do you?"

"I don't know anyone who specializes in Water Dogs," I confessed, "but I can ask around."

"That would be lovely," she said, sounding grateful.

"Ms. Tandy, thank you so much for this information. It's...it's really helpful."

"Well, I'm not normally one to talk out of school," she said.

"I don't think this counts," I said. "It's important that we entrust our dogs to people who are...well, worthy of that trust."

"Yes, it sure is."

"You take care," I said.

"Thank you," she said, and the line went dead.

"Well, that's suspicious," I said. "Whatever can it mean?"

Jack looked at me, and the look on his face was as puzzled as I felt.

twenty-one

We arrived at the hotel bone-tired and sick of the road. I was also literally nauseous, which I suspected had something to do with the microwave burrito I had consumed at our brief stop in Santa Ana. Old Blue had performed like a trooper, however, and I was eager to give her a rest.

Bree went to stretch her legs as Jack checked us in. I collapsed in a heap in a faux-Victorian-style chair in the garish lobby. The entire first floor of the hotel reminded me of Las Vegas—a showy, tasteless display of artificial luxury. If I rubbed off the gold paint, I knew I would find plywood underneath.

My attention was caught by Jack raising his voice. That was unusual. Jack was just about the mellowest person I had ever met. I groaned, got to my feet and walked over to the reception desk. I came up beside him and leaned on the desk heavily. "What's going on?"

"Booking snafu, apparently," he said. The woman behind the counter was studying her computer screen, her face completely impassive.

"How so?" I asked.

"I booked three rooms last night. They say I only booked two."

"What does your email say?" I asked.

Jack fished out his phone and found the email. He deflated. "Two," he said weakly.

"Ah," I said.

"I'm sorry," Jack apologized to the woman. "I thought for sure I'd gotten three. I'm so sorry. And I'm sorry for losing my temper."

The woman's face was as cold as granite. She wasn't buying the apology.

"Geez," Jack said, staring at his phone and shaking his head.

"If I didn't know you better, I'd say you were being sneaky," I said.

"What do you mean?"

"Oh dear, Casey. I guess we'll just have to share a room!" I said, waving my hand with exaggerated movements.

"I would never do that," he said.

"Do you have another room?" I asked the woman.

She didn't answer, but Jack said, "No, they're booked up for the dog show. I was probably lucky to get the rooms I did last night."

"The two rooms are fine," I said to the woman. I turned to Jack. "I'll room with Bree."

"Are you sure?" he asked.

"What are our options?" I asked. "Get another hotel? Or you could room with Bree."

"Egad," Jack said.

"Maybe I can convince her to take a shower," I said.

"It may be breaking some personal code," Jack suggested.

I shrugged.

"Are you sure you wouldn't rather share a room with me?" Jack asked.

"Why, Father Jack, if word were to get out, wouldn't your parishioners be scandalized?"

"Maybe a few of the elderly people," Jack conceded. "But not most. As I told you, we're liberal Christians. A quarter of our parishioners are gay or lesbian, and another quarter are living with a partner without being married. Actually, I think they'd be delighted."

"Hmpf," I said. But I grabbed his sweater and pulled him down to my level, planting a kiss on those gorgeous, angular lips of his. "Another time. When it's just us."

"Okay," he said. I could hear the disappointment in his voice, but I was relieved that he was willing to leave it there.

"How many room cards will you need?" the stoic woman behind the desk asked.

"Just one for one room, and two for the other," I said.

She nodded without looking at me and programmed the cards, sticking them into a small machine one at a time. That done, she put the cards into holders, wrote the room numbers on the holders, and put them on the desk. "Check out time is 11:00am on Sunday. Enjoy your stay."

"Thank you," Jack said, picking up the card holders. He handed two of them to me. "And again, I am sorry."

The woman flashed a false smile but did not meet Jack's eyes. Instead, she spun away and walked into the back room.

"Is it just me or did the temperature drop ten degrees?" I asked.

"I said I was sorry," Jack mumbled.

"You did. No need to grovel."

"But I feel like groveling."

"That's what church will do to you," I teased.

"'We acknowledge and bewail our manifold sins and wickedness,'" Jack said, affecting a dramatic tone.

"Is that a quote?" I asked.

"Prayer for public confession from the 1662 *Book of Common Prayer*," Jack said.

"See?"

"'I am a worm and no man,'" he mock-wailed. "Psalm 22."

"That's enough," I said. "Let's get the bags."

twenty-two

Normally I would think it lazy to just eat at the hotel restaurant. After all, we were in San Diego—no slouch in the culinary department. We were literally surrounded by exquisite dining opportunities. But no—here we were at the Traveler's Inn dining room, ordering from greasy, yellowed menus that made me long for hand-sanitizer.

But we had just driven for nearly twelve hours—so perhaps we could be forgiven. All I wanted to do was fill my belly and fall into bed.

The menu was a blur. I looked for the least-unhealthy option and settled on an el pastor tostada with guacamole and chipotle salsa. Jack ordered enchiladas, and Bree ordered waffles with apples, caramel sauce, and whipped cream.

No wonder she wears a muumuu, I thought, and instantly chastised myself for it. Somewhere along the way, I had stopped noticing her body odor quite as much. I did notice the waitress' nostrils twitching as she took our order, however.

"So tomorrow is the show," Jack said. "There certainly are a lot of dogs about."

There weren't any dogs in the restaurant, but he was right. Every time we'd stepped into the hall, we passed some or another gorgeous specimen of canine.

"Makes me wish we'd brought Tripod and Scout," Jack said.

"Are those your dogs?" Bree asked, her tired face brightening.

"Tripod is my dog—he has three legs, thus, Tripod," Jack smiled. "He's just a mutt, but I love him. Scout is Casey's dog."

"Scout—what a great dog name," Bree said, reaching for her water glass. I watched with amazement as she drained the whole thing in one gulp, leaving only the ice, and only some of that. She wiped her mouth and instantly became pensive. "But what happens when we get back home?" Bree asked. "I can't keep him—Abelard, I mean."

"We have a lot of options," I said, as comfortingly as I could. "Let's cross that bridge when we come to it."

"All right," Bree said, but she didn't sound too sure.

When our food arrived, I was pleasantly surprised that it was as fresh and tasty as it was. Jack dug in with gusto, and Bree demolished her waffles before I had eaten halfway through my tostada.

"I'm tired," Bree said, wiping syrup off her chin and throwing her napkin onto her empty plate.

"No kidding," I said, taking another crunchy bite of tostada.

"I think I'm going to go back to the room," Bree said.

"Do you have your card?" Jack asked.

She fished in the pocket of her muumuu and held it up. "See you in a bit," she said to me.

But before she could get up to leave, I asked no one in particular, "You know what would feel really good?"

"No, what?" Jack responded, right on cue.

"A hot shower. Doesn't that sound lovely?"

"I'm opting for a hot bath and a crossword puzzle," Jack said.

"That sounds lovely, too," I said. "What do you think, Bree? You could go first." I instantly froze, wondering if I had overstepped my bounds. Jack raised one eyebrow, one side of his magnificent lips curling into an almost-smile.

"Oh, I don't know. I don't like water much," Bree said, scooting out of her chair.

"The cats are rubbing off on you," Jack said.

"That's probably it. I'll commune with the Ascended Masters, read a bit from the Akashic records, and then hit the hay."

"Give my regards to the Lord Maitreya," Jack said.

"If he's around. I'm more likely to bump into Saint Germaine."

"He's not, strictly speaking, a Theosophical Master," Jack said, a little surprised.

She shrugged. "I can't help who hangs out at the library."

"Funny, that's just what I say about church," Jack said.

Bree smiled a tired smile. "I haven't said thank you yet. I am so grateful that you care about my sister's dog so much."

"You're welcome, Bree," I said.

She turned and shuffled off toward the room. I waited until she was out of earshot.

"Well, it was worth making the suggestion," I said.

Jack laughed, almost lowering his nose to his plate. When he sat back up again, he sighed. "You crack me up, Case."

"Well, I'm glad I entertain you."

"You do more than that. You delight me."

I reached for his hand and gave it a squeeze.

"You wanna come to my room and make out?" he asked.

"What are we, in high school?" I asked, feeling heat rise to my cheeks.

"You're only as old as you feel."

"Well, keep your teenage hormones in check for the time being," I said. "I'm afraid I'd start snoring in the middle of a kiss."

"That would be awkward," Jack conceded.

"Thank you for coming with me," I said, suddenly turning serious. I scooted over and put my head on his shoulder.

"Are you kidding? This is the most fun I've had since the sacristy flooded."

I narrowed one eye at him. "I'm not sure how to take that."

"Take it with the humor that was intended," he said, and kissed my hair. The make-out session was sounding better and better. But reason prevailed.

"I'm going to take that shower and turn in," I said.

"Sleep well," he said.

"Are you going to bed?" I asked.

"Soon enough. I think I'm going to go over to the bar, order a whiskey, and use my phone to read up on Theosophical metaphysics."

"Ah. Well, to each their own."

"I'll be asleep in a half hour, is what I'm saying," he grinned.

I kissed his shoulder and began to stand up. He caught me and pulled me back. I turned and found his beautiful lips on mine. I melted into them and felt a warm flood cascading over my brain and shoulders. After a timeless moment, his lips pulled back and he said, "Good night, Doctor."

"Good night, Father."

I stood up, before the temptation to join him in a drink—and possible fornication—could exert any more influence. I took one wrong turn on my way back to the room, but I finally found it. I put my key card to the pad beside the door and waited for the click. I pushed open the door, only to find Bree already in bed. The problem was, she wasn't alone. Two cats were curled up beside her.

"Uh, Bree," I said, turning on the light. "Where did the cats come from?"

"Found them..." she mumbled.

"You found them on the way back to the room?" I asked, my voice rising in incredulity.

"Un-hun," she said, turning over. "G'night."

twenty-three

I stumbled out of the hotel room and into the lobby in a desperate search for coffee. Somehow I found a carafe and poured myself a large celluloid cup of the life-giving liquid. It was too hot to drink just yet; more's the pity. I thought about adding more milk just to make it drinkable. Ice, I thought, and made my way to the ice machine. Picking up the metal scoop, I retrieved a couple of cubes and dropped them into my cup. Then I nearly jumped out of my skin.

"Hey, Case," Jack said. "Oh. Sorry. Didn't mean to startle you."

I closed my eyes and took a deep breath. "No, it's good. Adrenaline is quicker than caffeine, anyway."

"Oh. Well, in that case, glad to oblige." His beautiful lips turned up in a smile, and he leaned down and kissed me. "Good morning. How did you sleep?"

"Like a rock. My ass is sore, though."

"It was a long trip yesterday."

"That's for sure."

"Come with me, so I can get some coffee too?" He pointed to the lobby.

"Sure," I said. We started to walk.

"How was it with Bree?"

"Uh...weird. When I got back to the room, she was asleep. There were two cats with her."

He stopped. "How in the world?"

"That's not the weird part," I said. "When I woke up, there were four."

"Four cats?" Jack asked, his jaw dropping open.

"Uh...yeah. I know spontaneous generation was disproven by Louis Pasteur in the nineteenth century, but I'm beginning to think his findings were premature."

Jack laughed as he poured himself a cup. "Where on earth did they come from?"

I shrugged. "Maybe she's just a cat magnet."

"Is that a clinical diagnosis?"

"I'm not a *human* doctor..." I hedged.

"If anything begs for a cross-disciplinary approach, this does," Jack opined.

"The only thing I can think of is that in the middle of the night, she got up and went out and picked up a couple of strays."

Jack added some cream to his coffee. "I wonder..."

"What?" I asked.

"Bree said she hasn't left her apartment in seventeen years, right? So where did her cats come from? I'll bet, as far as she's concerned, she just woke up and there was a new cat...or two, over and over. I think she's a sleepwalker."

"I shudder to think of Bree, unconscious, roaming the streets of Davis in her muumuu at three in the morning," I confessed.

"And yet..."

"No, it's a good theory," I said.

"Should we take her some coffee?" he asked.

So we did. Jack waited outside while I went in. Bree was awake, sitting up in bed, stroking the cats. I handed her a steaming cup. "I brought you some coffee. I have sugar and creamers in my pocket."

"Oh, bless you," she said.

"That's Jack's job," I quipped.

"I'll just bet it is," she quipped back.

"Do you want to get some breakfast?" I asked.

"Oh, yes."

"We'll meet you in the dining room," I said.

I met Jack back in the hall, his eyebrows raised in query.

"I didn't ask, and she didn't say. But she acted like it was completely normal."

Jack shook his head. "That is so, so weird."

"Is there anything about Bree that isn't?"

"Point," Jack said. "And yet...I like her. A lot. She has a *Harold & Maude* quality—thinking of Maude, not Harold."

"I get it." I pointed toward the restaurant. "Breakfast?"

We were halfway through our omelets when Bree joined us. She ordered waffles again and an orange juice.

"So, uh, Bree, Casey and I were wondering...how did you come by your cats?" Jack asked with miserably fake nonchalance.

Bree did not seem to notice. "Oh, I just woke up, and there they were."

"Uh-huh," Jack said, nudging me with his elbow.

"It happens all the time."

Her orange juice arrived and she drank it down in one gulp. It was impressive, but again, weird.

"So what's the plan?" Jack asked.

I rolled my eyes.

"What?" Bree asked.

"He always has to have a plan," I complained.

"It's good to have a plan," Jack defended himself. "Otherwise, you don't know what you're doing."

"Sometimes it's good not to know what you're doing," I countered. "That way you're open to the unexpected."

"You're cute, the two of you," Bree said.

"Uh...thanks," I said.

"You must have something in mind," Jack said in my direction.

"Yes. We're going to go to the dog show."

"Check," Jack said, holding up his index finger.

"We're going to have a good time—or at the very least, we are going to look like we're having a good time," I continued.

"Check," Jack added his middle finger.

"We're going to watch the Boxers compete," I said.

"We are?" Jack asked.

"Why in the world would we come all the way to a dog show and not watch the Boxers compete?" I asked.

"Uh...I guess we wouldn't," Jack said, sounding a bit defeated.

"The Boxers show at 9:00, so we need to get going. The Shepherds show at 11:00. After the Boxers, we'll find the tent where the German Shepherds are getting ready. Either before the competition or after, Bree will introduce herself to Teal and will meet her new dog."

Bree pointed a spoon at me. "You make me nervous when you talk like that."

"I didn't say you were going to take him home, just that you own him."

"Okay, then." Her waffles arrived and she attacked them with impressive ferocity.

"And as I said before, we'll watch and listen. We'll talk to people—especially other people employing Teal."

"Okay," Jack said. "That's still nebulous, but I can get my head around it."

"Good boy," I said, patting his arm. To my amazement, Bree had finished her waffles.

"Shall we?" I asked, standing up. "Oh, and Bree...there will be hundreds of dogs there. No cats, please."

twenty-four

The day was warm, but overcast. We navigated into the parking lot, driving past row after row of RVs, Fifth-Wheelers, and trailers. Finally finding the lot reserved for regular autos, we parked the car and headed for the gate.

We were instantly caught up in the carnival atmosphere of the dog show. This time Jack navigated it like a pro. Dogs were everywhere. Just as we paid for our tickets, Bree froze as a Rhodesian Ridgeback began sniffing at her.

"Bree, are you all right?" I asked.

"I think I forgot to tell you. I'm afraid of dogs."

I'm sure my eyebrows jumped off my head. "Seems like something you might have warned us about."

"Do you know why you're afraid of dogs?" Jack asked.

"I was attacked by a dog when I was little," Bree said.

"Oy," I said under my breath.

Jack was more compassionate. "That little girl is still in you, but you're a lot more than her now."

"Is that a crack about my weight?" Bree scowled. She was

still standing motionless. The Ridgeback, however, had moved on.

"No!" Jack protested as I handed him his ticket. "I'm saying the adult Bree can comfort the child Bree, can tell her it's safe."

"But I'm not at all sure it's safe," she said. She did, in fact, appear frozen to the spot. I grabbed her elbow and led her away from the ticket booth so that we could continue the unfortunate revelations without impeding others.

"You do great with cats," I said.

"Yes, well, they're *cats*," she almost squealed.

"You do well with women and men, don't you?" I asked. "You get along fine with Jack, don't you?"

"Eh...yes, I suppose so." She eyed me suspiciously. "What's your point?"

"I know dogs and cats pretty well. Cats are inherently feminine, regardless of actual gender. Dogs are inherently masculine. It might help if you think of them as feminine and masculine expressions of the same kind of animal."

A thoughtful look crossed Bree's face. "Oh. They're just...men."

"Yeah," I said. "Instead of women."

She looked around, a look of wonder replacing her trepidation. "Oh. I guess it's okay, then." And at that, she struck out into the teeming mass of humans and dogs.

"Nice work," Jack said. "If the vet gig goes south, you could always become a therapist...or a priest."

"Not on your Jesus-loving life," I said. "I can't see her anymore."

"That striped muumuu is hard to miss," Jack said, "but you're right...I don't see her either."

"We could just follow the smell," I said.

Jack mock-punched my shoulder. "You're terrible."

"Forgive me, father, for I have sinned."

"You have to actually be penitent," he said. "And I very much doubt that you are."

We waded into the stream of people ourselves.

It didn't take long to find Bree. She was standing beside one of the rings, watching the pugs trotting around. "They're adorable," she said, as soon as she noticed me.

"They're good dogs," I said. "A genetic train-wreck in the nose department, but sweet."

"You would attract more good things into your life if you weren't so negative," Bree said without taking her eyes off the pugs.

"New Thought," Jack whispered. I had no idea what that meant, so I ignored him. I glanced at my watch. "Yikes! Boxers are up in five. Let's go!" I pulled the program out of my pocket to check the location of the ring and then headed out. I assumed Jack and Bree would follow and was relieved to see that they did.

When we finally got to the ring, we had missed the males, but we were in time for the bitches, and took seats in the fifth row of the risers. It was lucky that the Boxers showed early—they typically do—because I knew seats would be harder to come by as the day wore on.

"Are they going to do tricks?" Bree asked.

"No, this is Conformation," I said. "It's like a beauty pageant. All they have to do is stand and trot and look pretty doing it."

"Oh." Bree cocked her head.

"That's *conformation*, not *confirmation*," Jack began, but I cut him off.

"Just stop," I said, swatting his leg.

"I learned that the hard way."

The first of the Boxers entered the ring, followed by the others. As they trotted around the circle, a loudspeaker cackled, and a pleasant female voice welcomed us to the Boxer competition.

I pointed to the first dog, a light-colored brindle. "The first bitch is Garden Party's Proud Mary. I've been following her for a while now." I had to consult the program for the second one. "Uh...the second there is Magic Moon's High Plains Drifter. I haven't seen her before."

"Are those names?" Bree asked. "Because those are some pretty weird names."

"Yes, and yes," I said. "Purebred names always include the name of the breeder's 'brand,' and nobody calls them by those names." I pointed. "Oh look! It's London Bridges Cowgirl Sally. Just to show you that no rule is hard and fast, they actually do call her Sally. So far, my money is on her."

"Uh...isn't that..." Jack pointed.

I froze. Leading the fourth dog was Austin Teal. "Holy cow," I said. I quickly adjusted. "Well...good. Let's see him in action. Bree, the man with the fawn-colored bitch there is Austin Teal. He's the guy we're here to see."

"Oh. Handsome," she said.

I did not dispute that. He was, in fact, ruggedly handsome. He had that cleft in his chin that some people have—some people that often left me weak in the knees. I steeled my resolve and watched him closely—not to admire his form, but to watch him perform.

He was, it was quickly clear, an excellent handler. His hand held the thin nylon show lead lightly, about six inches above his bitch's neck. His step was springy, matching the dog's own. The fawn bitch kept her eyes glued to him and anticipated his every move. They worked together like a well-oiled machine.

"I don't know anything about this, but he looks good," Jack said.

"He's very good," I said. "The bitch might be complete riffraff, but she'd have a chance with him."

"And is the...uh...it's hard for me to say 'bitch.' Is the...*dog* riffraff?" Jack asked.

"Ha! Coward," I poked him in the side. "But no, far from it. That is one beautiful Boxer. This is going to be a tight contest." The other contender was High Plains Drifter, a dark brindle with a perfect head. But it looked to me like her handler might also be her owner—in other words, good, but not a pro. Even though Drifter looked like the superior dog, my gut told me the win would go to Teal and his fawn bitch.

I was not mistaken. A blue ribbon was handed to Teal, and he praised the fawn bitch, who instantly began jumping up and down in place.

"Okay, he's the real deal," I said. "That's...comforting."

"Are you starting to rethink this?" Jack asked.

"No...not after the way he handled Anselm's death. It's just another piece of the puzzle. We haven't got the whole picture yet."

Jack nodded. "I enjoyed that. It was great."

"See there? You're getting hooked."

"When do the three-legged mutts show?" he asked.

I laughed again. "Dream on. But you could enter Tripod in obedience or rally. You'd both have a blast."

"What's rally?" he asked.

"Think of it as a timed obstacle course."

"Huh. Sounds fun," Jack said. I could see the wheels turning.

"I'm ready," Bree said.

"Are you nervous?" I asked.

"A little," she confessed. "I wish I had a cat to hold."

"Maybe we can find you a chihuahua," Jack joked.

I rolled my eyes. "She wants something to comfort her, not make her jump out of her skin." I put my hand on Bree's arm. "We're just hanging out and gathering information," I reminded her. "Let's go."

We started walking toward the pavilion housing the German Shepherds. I could see that Jack was enjoying the great variety of dogs. It was his second dog show, and it thrilled me that he was loving it.

"Won't Teal recognize you?" Jack asked. "Or me, for that matter? I mean, we were both there, when...you know...Anselm died."

"What if he does?" I asked. "The dog-show world is small. These people see each other at pretty much every show. Did you notice all those RV's we passed in the parking lot?"

"Yeah," Jack said. "What was that about?"

"Those are all people showing dogs. Some of them are retired, some are pros. They just travel from one show to the next."

"So they actually live in those?"

"I'm sure most of them have houses too, but yeah, for part of the year."

"There is a level of fanaticism here that most people don't notice," he pronounced.

"Tell me about it," I agreed.

"I think it's lovely," Bree said. "I'd love to have a trailer and go from cat show to cat show."

"Well, that's a thing," I said. "You could. They—" I was about to say "they reek to high heaven because of all the intact tomcats in one place," but decided against it. After all, Bree was not challenged by olfactory extremes.

"Cotton candy," Jack said, pointing at one of the concession stands. "Watermelon-flavored cotton candy."

"You want some cotton candy?" I asked, frowning at him.

"Who doesn't love cotton candy?"

"No ten-year-old I ever heard of," I said.

"My inner ten-year-old is dying for watermelon cotton candy," Jack said. "Do you mind?"

There was no line. I shrugged. "It's your teeth," I said.

He flashed me an adorably childlike smile and jogged over to the stand.

"Make it two, Jack," Bree called.

"You sure you don't want in?" Jack called over his shoulder at me.

"I'm holding out for the deep-fried Twinkies," I yelled.

"Really?" he stopped and faced me.

"No, not really."

"Oh. Okay," he turned and bought two bags of cotton candy. He jogged back and handed one to Bree.

"Oh, thank you," she said.

I rolled my eyes as they both ripped into their bags and began to tear tufts off the pink masses inside.

Jack extended a tuft toward me. "C'mon, you know you want a taste."

"I don't. But thanks," I said, with as much disgust as a face could muster.

"Suit yourself." He dug in.

We soon found the pavilion we were looking for, and as we stepped into its shade I waited for my eyes to adjust. Within a minute or two I could clearly see a vast sea of crates, lawn chairs, and grooming tables. It was also very loud, with hundreds of dogs yelping, barking, whining, and howling.

"Beautiful," Jack said, admiring one of the German Shepherds nearby. He licked cotton candy off of his fingers and put the rest of the bag into his back pocket.

"Aren't they?" I asked.

"There's that man," Bree said, pointing with a tuft of the candy.

I followed the tuft and saw who she meant. Teal was leaning over one of the crates. As he straightened up, I could see he was yelling.

There was too much noise to discern what he was yelling about, but his body language and red face were clear. I walked toward him as fast as I could manage. He had a plastic dog bowl in one hand, and I winced as he raised it over his head and brought it down on the wire crate in front of him. He bashed the crate repeatedly, and I heard Bree behind me yelp with distress—she saw it too.

"What the hell?" Jack wondered.

There was a German Shepherd inside the wire crate, and with every crash, I could see the startled dog jump.

"What's he so mad about?" Jack asked.

I didn't know, but no matter what it was, that was no way to treat a dog. It was also counterproductive—the dog would be such a nervous wreck after a display like that there's no way it would show well.

"He's a monster," I decided.

"No kidding," Jack said, catching up with me and putting one arm around my shoulder. We were about ten feet from Teal and the quivering dog. My eyes widened as I saw the name tag on the crate. I reached out and put a hand on Bree's wrist. "Bree, that dog he's yelling at—that's Abelard. That's *your dog*."

twenty-five

I knew that Bree had little love for her sister's dog—or for any dogs, for that matter. But when she actually *saw* Abelard—and saw the abuse Teal was dishing out—something must have snapped in her. Cool as an ice cube, almost in slow motion, she turned to me. "Tell me what to do," she said.

I nodded, my eyes flashing back and forth as I thought. Then I knew. "I'm going to go confront Teal for his abuse," I said. "I'm going to draw him away and distract him. Jack, it looks like he's got an assistant, and he does not look happy about this either. I need you to distract him."

"How?"

"I don't care. Tell him you're available for confession. Make something up. Just do it quick. Bree, as soon as both of them are distracted, go in there and get your dog."

"Do I need a leash?"

I pulled a show lead out of my pocket and handed it to her. "Just slip it over his head and get the hell out of the pavilion as fast as you can. Head for the parking lot. We'll catch up."

She nodded. I checked her eyes. They were steely with

anger and resolve. I looked at Jack. He was grinning like an idiot. He was enjoying this. Weird. "Okay, let's do this."

I headed straight for Teal. He was still yelling, both at Abelard and at his assistant. I didn't catch what he was so upset about. I didn't care. He didn't notice me until I was standing right in front of him.

He paused mid-yell and blinked. I could tell he recognized me but didn't know from where. Then his face shifted as he made the connection. "Uh...Doctor....?"

"Gibbons," I said, not smiling. "I need to talk to you privately."

"It will need to wait—" he began, but I stepped on his foot. Hard.

"Now," I said.

He was silent for a moment, and I imagined he had no idea what to make of me. Good. It would keep him on his toes—hopefully sore toes.

"Let's...go over there," he pointed at a patch of grass just beyond the north side of the pavilion that seemed reasonably free of people.

"After you," I said.

A puzzled, concerned look crossed his face, and he turned and headed for the edge of the big tent. I followed. I chanced a glance over my shoulder and saw Jack with his arm around the shoulder of Teal's assistant, leading him in another direction and...were they praying? I shook my head and focused on Teal.

He cleared the pavilion and continued another ten paces. In the relatively clear space, I continued past him and then turned—I needed him facing away from the pavilion, after all. As I had hoped, he turned with me. I jutted out my hip, crossed my arms, and glared at him.

"What is this about?" he said, betraying his impatience.

"Do you know the American Kennel Club's Code of Ethics for Registered Handlers?" I asked.

He blinked. "What?"

"Because I do. I know them by heart," I said.

"I don't have time for this," he said. "I'm due in the ring in five minutes."

"Here is the first one," I said, piercing him with my gaze. "I vow to ensure that the welfare of the dogs in my care is a priority, not only at dog shows but at home and on the road. Their well-being, security, and safety is to be placed above all other business considerations. The ultimate responsibility for the dogs cannot be transferred to assistants or others."

"I don't know what you're going on about, but I have a job to do."

He turned to go, but I jumped in his path and balled my fists. "Unless you want me to report you to the superintendent of the show—and unless you want to suspend your business while the Ethics Review Board investigates my complaint—you'll stay right where you are."

His face bunched up in a mask of malevolence. "Are you threatening me, Doctor?"

"Not at all. I'm giving you the facts. I saw the way you treated that dog back there. I'm sure that both the Superintendent and the Ethics Review Board will be very interested."

"It will be my word against yours," he said.

"And the word of the two friends with me, who also witnessed it. And I predict that your assistant will not be eager to be in the line of fire either. I'm betting on his cooperation."

"You wouldn't," he said.

"In a heartbeat," I said. "Now, the way I see it, you have one chance to avoid a complaint. You can justify—to my satisfaction—the display of anger that I just witnessed. What could possibly explain your treatment of that dog?"

I chanced a glance over his shoulder and, to my great relief, saw Bree leading a German Shepherd away toward the parking lot. A part of me relaxed. I reminded myself to be vigilant. I returned my gaze to Teal.

He stepped toward me and leaned down until his nose was almost touching mine. Then, gritting his teeth, he said, "I don't answer to you." Then he turned and stormed away.

"No, you don't," I said. "But you will."

twenty-six

As soon as I saw Teal reenter the pavilion, I began to jog toward the parking lot. I was out of breath by the time I caught up with Bree and the dog. Looking around, I saw Jack making his way toward us, speed-walking. He waved. I grinned and waved back. I looked toward the German Shepherd pavilion and allowed myself to relax a bit, seeing that we were out of the direct line of sight. Unless Teal had followed us— and there was no evidence that he had—we were in the clear.

I knelt by Abelard and gave him a quick checkup. He appeared to be unharmed and was clearly glad for my attention. "Who's a pretty boy?" I said.

"He actually seems nice," Bree said, sounding genuinely surprised.

"He's a lovely, lovely dog. And German Shepherds have great temperaments, generally."

Jack finally caught up to us, and I was annoyed that he didn't seem to be out of breath at all. "I think I won a convert."

"Really?" I asked. "And is that a good thing?"

"I'm kidding," he said. "The guy couldn't wait to get away from me."

"Did you get his name?" I asked. "We might need him as a witness."

"Not only that, I got his contact info," Jack said, holding up his phone.

"How did you do that?" I asked.

"Trade secrets," he said.

I narrowed one eye at him.

"Oh! He's making a poopy," Bree said, her voice rising with distress.

"Better here than in the car," I said.

"But I don't have anything to clean it up with," she objected.

"Well, normally it's bad form to leave any scat at a show," I said. "But...there are circumstances, you know."

"So we'll just leave it?" Bree asked. She looked as guilty as I felt about it.

"Let's get out of here," I said, "Before Teal discovers the dog is missing and someone comes looking for us."

"Uh...Case," Jack said. He appeared to be staring at his feet. I looked at his feet, and realized he was actually staring at the feces.

"Yeah?"

"You might...want to take a look at this." He squatted and bent down for a closer look at the feces.

"We don't really have time for this," I said.

"I think we do," he said.

I groaned in exasperation and walked back to where he was. I squatted and looked at the pile of poop.

Except that it wasn't a pile. It was a pool of dark brown mucus. And swimming in the middle of that pool was what looked like an intact sausage. "What the hell?" I asked no one in particular.

Jack fished the cotton candy from his back pocket and stuffed the rest of it into his mouth.

"Poop makes you...hungry?" I asked, scowling at him.

He ignored me and used the empty plastic bag to gather up the sausage and as much of the mucus as he could. He twisted the bag's top and held it up. "Okay, now we can go."

twenty-seven

It was a long, long drive back to Davis. After nearly 700 miles, it was deep in the night when we exited the offramp. I was grateful that I had Jack to trade off driving duties with me. Bree volunteered to take a turn, but since she hadn't been behind the wheel in nearly thirty years, and did not have a driver's license, I nixed that right out of the gate.

One happy accident of the trip was that Bree and Abelard got to share the back seat the whole way, and although Bree was uncertain about dogs to begin with, by the end of the trip she and Abelard had definitely bonded.

I looked back and saw them asleep in a pile and smiled. Jack noticed and looked over his shoulder. "I'm not sure you could separate them now," he said.

"There is the matter of the cats," I said.

"Right," he agreed.

Bree heard us talking and stirred, emitting a languorous yawn. "Are we there yet?" she asked.

"Almost," I answered. The dark thought that had been circling my brain for the last hundred miles lit on my tongue.

"Uh...Bree...I don't want to alarm you, but I doubt Teal is going to give up so easily. He's a monster, but...there's got to be another reason he wants to keep this dog."

"The scat may give us a clue to that," Jack said.

That was true, but we wouldn't know anything until I had a chance to get it into my lab at the clinic. And I sure as hell wasn't going to do that tonight. The only thing keeping my eyes open was Red Bull and necessity.

"What are you saying?" Bree asked.

"I'm saying...I'm not sure you're safe here."

"Why wouldn't I be?"

"I'm afraid Mr. Teal might come and try to retrieve Abelard."

"But you're taking him with you, aren't you?"

I looked at Jack. He smiled. We hadn't actually discussed that, but it was the only logical option. There's no way Abelard could peacefully cohabitate with twenty or more cats in a tiny apartment. Not if Bree wanted the cats to live. "Of course," I said.

"Well, how would he know I took him?" Bree asked. "I don't think he saw me, and even if he did, he doesn't know me from Eve."

I hoped that was true. "But, just in case, how do you feel about staying in a hotel for a couple of nights?" I asked.

"No," she said. "I'd miss my babies. Besides...." She looked out the window.

"I'd be glad to pay for it," Jack said.

I watched her face in the rear-view mirror. Jack had nailed it. "No, but thank you, Jack. I want to go home."

"Okay," I said. And just like that, we were there. I waited a moment before turning off the engine, staring at the decrepit apartment building. It was 2:55am, and it was dark and lifeless. If anyone was waiting to surprise Bree, they were doing it very quietly.

Before I could get out, Bree slid from the back seat and gave Abelard a nuzzle. "You be a good boy." Then she moved to Jack's window. He rolled it down.

"Do you want us to come in with you?" he asked.

"Nope. You go home and get some sleep. If the Millidor Empire has been up to no good, I don't want you to be in any danger."

"That's very thoughtful," Jack said.

"I'll call you," I said.

"Not if I call you first," Bree smiled, and then she turned and tottered off toward her apartment. I hit the brights to help illumine her way. And then she was in.

I sighed. "Am I just being paranoid?"

"I think you're exhibiting appropriate caution, given the circumstances," Jack said.

"You're very sweet," I said.

"It takes practice," Jack confessed. "But I try to practice every day." He watched my face. "Do you want me to go check in on her?"

"Would you hate me if I said yes?" I asked.

"I would...no, of course not," he said. He leaned over and kissed me, and then got out of the car. For some reason, Abelard whined to see him go. I turned and stroked the Shepherd's fur. I decided this was probably a good time for a potty break, so I attached his leash and led him from the car.

He was just finishing up when Jack returned. "All is well," he announced.

"Whew," I said. In moments, we were all reinstalled in our places and heading out to the highway.

"What about you?" Jack said.

"What about me?" I asked, indicating a left turn onto the onramp.

"Teal didn't see Bree, but he did see you. I don't think you should go home tonight...or maybe for a while."

Strangely, I hadn't thought of that. I had been so worried about Bree, that I hadn't considered my own safety at all. I wondered if that was some kind of flaw...one that might prove to be a fatal flaw one day.

"Where should I go?"

"Come stay with me," Jack said. Before I could object, he said, "The parsonage has a guest room, and Scout, Tripod, and Abelard would love it. What do you think?"

I wanted to object, but he was making sense. I could go to a hotel, but why? The people and animals I care about would all be at his place. If I couldn't be home, I wanted to be there.

"No funny stuff," I said.

"What are you talking about?"

"I'm talking about sex," I said.

"Of course not. I mean, not until you're ready," he said. "Have I ever pressured you?"

He hadn't, of course. The only pressure I felt was internal. I knew he was willing, but that was...welcome, pleasurable, exciting. I didn't know why I was so hesitant. And then I remembered. *He's a freaking priest!* the voice in my head reminded me. *With great lips,* I reminded the voice. *And an even better heart.*

"Sure," I said. "Let's go to your house. But first, let's collect the dogs."

I wasn't sure about all three dogs in the back seat, but after the initial excitement, they seemed to get along just fine. It was pretty crowded back there, and I heard one yelp, but when we arrived at Jack's rectory, everyone seemed to be in one piece and there was no blood. I considered it a win.

It might have been my imagination, but I thought I saw the faint pink glow of dawn in the East as we entered the gloomy house. It wasn't gloomy on the inside, though, but warm and cozy. The dogs chased each other and demanded to be fed, which seemed fair. As soon as I dished up their bowls, I sat heavily at the kitchen table.

Jack emerged from the spare room, his face relaxed in a tired smile. "It's all ready for you," he said.

"Thanks," I said.

"They seem happy," he said, pointing at the dogs with his chin. The three of them were side-by-side, noses in bowls, chowing down.

"There's nothing so peaceful as the sound of livestock grazing," I said.

Jack laughed. He walked over to me, leaned down, and planted a quick, tender kiss on my lips. I grabbed his hand and held it to my cheek.

"I'm going to try to catch a couple of hours," Jack said.

"When is your first appointment tomorrow?" I asked.

"Ten," he said. "So I can sleep in a little. Good night." He kissed the top of my head and walked toward his bedroom. "I'm going to leave the door ajar so Tripod can get in," he called over his shoulder.

"Okay," I said. When he was gone, I helped myself to a whisky. By the time I had drained the grass, all three dogs were finished. I let them out the back, and in what seemed like mere seconds they had done their business. Abelard seemed to get the idea, too, I was relieved to see. Tripod disappeared into Jack's room.

I sighed and went to the guest room. I flipped on the light

and saw that, while the bed was a small single, and the room was clearly used for storage, it was tidy and not unwelcoming. I got undressed and slipped under the covers. Scout jumped up on the bed, although there was barely room for one. Abelard curled into a ball on the quilted rug.

But strangely, I couldn't sleep. Images from the past day raced through my brain. The question that wouldn't leave me alone was just what was in that baggie? What had Abelard pooped out, and why was it important? It would need to wait, of course, but I couldn't stop thinking about it.

Scout had taken over the bed by this point, and I didn't have the heart to push her off. Instead, without really thinking about it, I got up and went to Jack's room. I put a hand on his hip and shook him gently.

"Huh? What?" He looked up at me, and his sleepy eyes widened. It was dark, but I was clearly in my underwear and t-shirt. His face screwed up into a question.

"I don't want to...do anything," I said. "But will you hold me?"

His face melted into a compassionate smile. He shooed Tripod off the bed and thew back the covers. He patted the spot in front of him and I slid in, turning my back to him and marveling at how well we fit together and how good it felt. His arm pulled me tight against him; I felt his breath on my ear. I could smell the spicy odor of his body. It melted me.

In seconds, I was out.

twenty-eight

I don't remember a single second of my drive to work the next morning. I was positively drunk on unfamiliar chemicals, all of them flowing from the feeling of spooning with Jack. Waking up beside him, feeling his arm around me, smelling his skin...it was all I could do to keep my eyes open and on the road.

So what if he's a priest? the voice in my head reasoned. *So what if he's religious? He's not* crazy *religious.* Another voice in my head countered, *Have you forgotten that he talks to Jesus as if he were a real person? If that's not crazy, what is?* The first voice did not know what to say to that. I am a scientist, after all. Science and religion are supposed to be mortal enemies...aren't they? Suddenly, I wondered what Jack would have to say about that question. And the thing was...I really wanted to know. But in the next moment, none of that mattered as I imagined his magnificent lips on mine...

I was hot and bothered by the time I pulled into my space. I glanced in my rear-view mirror and found that I was flushed...

or blushing...or something. "Snap out of it, Doctor!" I told myself out loud.

I reached over to the passenger seat and picked up the paper bag containing Abelard's scat. Then I got out of the car and went to work.

I wanted to be there an hour earlier than anyone else, but I'd had so little sleep the night before that it just seemed impossible. Lack of sleep was probably also responsible for my fuzzy-headedness, I realized—it wasn't just about the hormones.

As soon as I walked in, one of Stacy's eyebrows raised at the sight of me. She didn't say anything, but I did wonder what she was thinking. It couldn't have been good. I went to the bathroom and looked in the mirror.

"Oh." There hadn't been enough real estate on the rear-view mirror to see the tragic state of my hair. I fished around in the cupboard, found a dog brush, and quickly applied it, arm-wrestling my bird's nest into submission. I was only partially successful.

I needed to talk to Ellie, but I really didn't want Stacy to catch wind of it. Coming out of the bathroom, I hovered just within sight of Ellie's desk and waved until I caught her eye. Her eyebrows rose in surprise, then she looked over her shoulder—no doubt looking to see where Stacy was before giving anything away—then she rose and rounded the corner toward me.

"What's up?" she whispered.

"Can you clear any of my appointments without Stacy knowing about it?"

"Probably. Are you okay?" Her eyes wandered to my hair.

"I'm fine."

"Did you sleep in a dumpster?" she asked.

"Never mind where I slept," I said.

That made her grin. "You don't say."

"Just...get me some time, can you?"

"No problem, boss." She waggled her eyebrows at me and said, "Rawr!" before returning to her desk.

I wanted to call after her, "It's not what you think," but Stacy would have heard. And besides that, it was *almost* what she was thinking...just not the funnest bits.

I grabbed the folder from the rack for my first client. A voice in my head simply could not keep quiet. *Do I want to sleep with Jack?* Another voice clarified, *You mean, do you want to have sex with Jack?* The first voice said, *No need to be so crude.* The second voice said, *That's not crude, that's real. And you haven't answered the question.* The problem was, I didn't know what I wanted from the relationship—or if I wanted a relationship at all. A part of me was still smarting from my divorce. Sure, it had been five years ago, but it had also been emotionally brutal. *What do you want from Jack?* the first voice asked.

"Just...shut up," I said aloud, pausing by the door to Exam Room Two.

I opened the door and found myself facing a coon hound and a very guilty-looking owner. "Mr. ...Braun. Hi, I'm Doctor Gibbons." I shook the man's hand. He was dressed like a farmer, in baggy utility trousers and a red-checked flannel shirt. A battered straw cowboy hat rested on an empty chair.

"Pete."

"Nice to meet you, Pete. Who do we have here?" I asked.

The hound had a red bandana tied tightly around its tail. "That's Mary. I...God, I didn't mean to, but I...caught her tail in the door. I heard something snap."

"Ouch," I said. "Let's take a look. Can you hold her head and keep her calm?" I asked. I wondered if I should ask one of our techs or assistants to join us, but Pete stepped up and seemed to have a good grip on Mary.

As I gingerly peeled back the bandana, fresh blood dripped onto the linoleum floor. The redness of the bandana had concealed just how soaked with blood it actually was. I rose and snagged some gauze, cotton, and chlorhexidine.

Sitting cross-legged, I worked as quickly as I could, clipping away the fur, cleaning the wound, and dressing it. Every now and then Mary emitted a whine, and I cooed at her softly as I worked, patting her haunches now and then.

"Okay," I said, standing up. "That will take care of the blood."

"How bad is it?" Pete asked.

"Well, it isn't severed, but she did bang it up pretty good."

Pete hung his head. "I banged it up."

"You didn't mean to," I said.

"No," he agreed.

"Accidents happen, and it isn't going to help Mary if you beat up on yourself. You need to focus on her, not on you."

That seemed to snap him out of it. "Uh...yeah...of course."

"There's not much we can do for damaged tails. You've got two choices. We can cut it off, just shy of the damage—that's probably the safest route."

His eyes got big. "And what's the other choice?"

I shrugged. "Do nothing and see if it heals up. I can send you home with some antibiotics to keep it from getting infected. But it will probably be really painful for a while—and of course, she can't help but knock it on everything she passes. Wagging will hurt too. And she might end up with a permanent kink in the tail."

"So...my two choices are to lop it off, or to just let it be and hope that it heals?"

"That's it." And then one of the voices in my head said, *Those are your choices when it comes to Jack, too.* I felt a swoon of vertigo. End the relationship, or just let it be and hope that it...

that I...heal. I took a deep breath and steadied myself on the exam table.

Mr. Braun had said something, but I had missed it. "Sorry, I was lost in thought," I said, shaking my head. "What was that?"

"What do you recommend?"

I opened my mouth to say *Lop it off*, but some deep and primal part of me that believed in sympathetic magic wouldn't permit it. "Let's...leave it be and see how she does," I said. "The cut will heal. She might have a kink, but if it bothers her, we can always cut it off later."

He nodded. "Okay."

I felt my heart wrench in my chest. *Let's leave it be and see how she....how I...do.*

twenty-nine

All day I kept hoping for a chance to examine that baggie, and all day it kept not happening. Ellie did indeed clear an hour for me—only to have it usurped by an emergency walk-in. I was all set to skip lunch to get at it, but then Stacy announced that a cat with a maggot-infested abscess was on its way in. Joy.

Glancing at the clock, I saw that it was nearly 5:00pm, and I still had two clients to see. My phone buzzed and I glanced at the text. "What did you find?" It was from Jack.

"No time yet. Want to come down? Off at 6."

I put the phone back in the pocket of my lab coat and sighed. Two more. I grabbed the folder from the rack and plunged in.

———

It was actually 6:15 when my last client left with her limping Lhasa-apso, looking for all the world like a lame, canine Cousin It. I handed the file folder to Stacy, who nodded in the direction of the waiting room. I looked up and saw Jack rising from the couch, setting aside the battered *Dog Fancy* magazine from three years ago.

"C'mon back," I said to him. Stacy turned to face me, her eyebrows raised over her cat's-eye glasses. To her credit, she did not object out loud. Every now and then she remembered who worked for whom.

Jack walked around the desk and bent down to kiss me. I put up my hand. "Not at work," I whispered.

"Oh. All right. I thought you were off."

"I am. Just...I can't be that vulnerable here."

"Oh. Weird. But okay." He looked a little hurt. I decided he was a big boy and he'd adjust.

"I've been keeping the sample in the refrigerator," I said.

"Right next to the yogurt?" he asked.

"We do have a dedicated refrigerator for potential biohazards," I said.

"Sounds prudent," he said.

I put on a pair of blue nitrile gloves and opened the small silver refrigerator. I grabbed the baggie, which looked even more gross than it had the day before.

"I think there's still some cotton candy in there," Jack said, pointing at a tiny tuft of pink. "Watermelon, remember? It was good."

I have a theory that there is a part of the male brain that is eternally twelve years old. Jack was providing important anecdotal evidence of this.

I wiped down the workspace next to the microscope with one hand as I held the baggie in the other. Fortunately, it wasn't leaking. I gingerly set it down and grabbed a scalpel.

"Can I watch?" Ellie asked, speed-walking up to us.

"Sure," I said.

"What is it?" she asked.

"We don't know yet," I answered.

I set the scalpel aside and untwisted the baggie, finding the opening and widening it. While I did that, I filled Ellie in on our adventure in San Diego. Fortunately for me, Jack picked up the narrative when I got distracted.

"And the dog pooped out *this*?" Ellie asked.

"I watched him do it. Ringside seat," Jack answered.

I picked up the scalpel and began to examine the sausage-shaped object swimming in the now-congealed brown mucus.

Jack and Ellie leaned in, until all three of our heads were nearly touching.

"It's a condom," Jack said. "See? That's the reservoir tip, there."

I saw it. "And over here, it's tied off—twice." I pointed to the other end of it. Where there would normally have been a thick band of latex, the condom had been cut about five millimeters past the final knot.

"A dog pooped out a condom," I said.

"So what's in the condom?" Jack asked.

I made an incision in the condom, and using a pair of tweezers, peeled the latex back a bit. "Don't breath," I said. "Back away. Now."

I held my breath and followed my own orders, waving Jack and Ellie away. I motioned them toward the front desk, which was around the corner.

"It looked like a white powder," Jack said.

"Exactly," I said.

"But what was it?" Ellie asked.

"It could be Anthrax or Ricin," I said. "If Anselm was carrying around one of those condoms in his belly, too—"

"And if it broke open..." Jack continued. "Could it look like what we saw?"

"I don't know," I said. "I'm not an expert on biochemical weapons. I can do some research, though."

"But why would someone feed a dog a condom full of poison?" Ellie asked. "Why not just slip the dog some snail and slug pellets? Dogs scarf them up like kibble."

It was a good question.

"Maybe it's not poison, as such," Jack suggested. "Maybe it's drugs. Heroin, maybe."

"That would make sense," I said. Then the light bulb went on. "Teal shows in Mexico. *Abelard* showed in Mexico, just before the San Diego show."

Jack nodded. Ellie's eyes were wide.

"But if it was heroin, would the dog have the same reaction?" Jack asked.

I nodded. "Oh, yeah. With a dose like that, it might as well be Anthrax," I said.

"But we still don't know for sure what it is," Ellie said.

"No, but regardless of what it is, it could be really, really dangerous. We don't want to accidentally breath this stuff."

"What are you going to do?" Jack asked.

"Well, the fact that we're not all thrashing on the floor and foaming at the mouth already is a plus." I peered around the corner at the counter, at the baggie, at the...whatever it was. "Ellie, can you grab me a biohazard bag? I'm going to hold my breath and bag that up again."

"And then what are you going to do with it?" Jack asked.

"Well, we don't have the equipment or protective gear to do a chemical analysis of it here. So, we need to take it to someone who does. Thing is, I'm not sure who that is."

"So...?" Jack asked, one eyebrow raised.

"So...I'm going to take it to Gus."

thirty

Jack insisted on coming with me. As Ellie and I closed up shop, I mused about whether he was motivated more by jealousy or by a protective impulse. *Why choose?* the voice in my head asked. I was slightly ashamed of myself for enjoying the thought that he might be jealous—but only very slightly. I put the biohazard into a discarded brown paper lunch bag and folded the top over several times.

I paused by the door and sent Gus a text. "Can you meet up right now?" Then I waved to Stacy, not bothering to pause long enough to discern whether she was glaring at me or not. Jack and I walked out to the parking lot.

"Let's take one car," Jack said. "We can swing back here on the way home."

By home he meant *his* home, which was fine. That was where Scout was, anyway. And in truth, for me, home is wherever Scout is. "Okay," I said, walking around to the passenger side of Jack's Mini Cooper.

I put the paper bag on the floorboard and climbed in. My pocket vibrated and I pulled out my phone. "Gus is at Millie's."

"Millie's it is, then," Jack said, making a left out of the parking lot.

My mind raced as I considered our discovery. I searched for anthrax and ricin on my phone and discovered that if we had breathed in any spores of either toxin, we wouldn't know for about 72 hours, at which time we would be goners. Great.

"Uh...Case," Jack said.

I looked up at him, suddenly feeling a tinge of guilt for ignoring him. "Yeah?"

"Don't panic, and don't turn around, but... I'm probably just imagining it. But let's test it."

He barely slowed down to make a sudden right turn. "This isn't the way," I said.

"No, it isn't," he agreed, his eyes flitting to his rear-view mirror. His face was taut and pale.

"What is it?" I asked.

"I think we're being followed," he said.

I started to look over my shoulder, but Jack raised his voice. *"Don't look back!"* he repeated.

"Oh. Okay. Right." I settled back into my seat. "Who is it? Is it Teal?"

"The windshield is tinted," he said.

"Isn't that illegal?" I asked.

He didn't answer. Instead, he made a couple more random turns, taking us into the twisting hills surrounding Gold Valley.

"Is he still there?"

"Yep," Jack said through clenched teeth.

"Can you read the license plate?" I asked.

"There is no front license plate," he said.

"Huh. Isn't *that* illegal?" I asked again.

"I don't think this person is really concerned with legality," Jack said. "What should I do?"

"Just go to Millie's," I said. "I think I'll feel safer if there are more eyes around."

Jack nodded and somehow found his way back to the county road. In five minutes we were pulling into the parking lot at Millie's. "There he goes," Jack said. "License plate."

I whipped my head around and leaned toward Jack's side window, as if that would help me see more clearly. A black sedan with tinted windows continued on down the county road, quickly disappearing around a curve.

"I got EUH," I said. "But I didn't get the rest of it."

"They were California plates, but I got EVH, not EUH," Jack said.

"Damn," I said.

"Well, it's something," Jack said.

I got out of the car, grabbed the paper sack, and looked around, my senses tingling. "I feel very weird right now," I confessed.

Jack nodded and looked at me with sadness and concern in his eyes. "My life was pretty boring until I met you," he said.

"I'm not sure how to take that," I said, grateful for the levity.

"Just a simple statement of fact," he said. "Now I have a three-legged dog and I seem to be in dangerous situations on a semi-regular basis."

"And?" I shut the car door.

"Keeps a fella on his toes," Jack said.

He was trying to keep it light, but I could tell he was whistling in the dark. He was rattled. His hands were shaking. I took his left hand in mine and squeezed it. "We're okay," I said.

"We're okay," he repeated.

I led him to the door of the diner and went in. Sarge waved us over to the counter where, sure enough, Gus was poised with a cup of coffee. He was in street clothes, which must mean I caught him on his day off. He rose to greet us, and I could tell he was not pleased to see Jack. Still, he was cordial and shook his hand. I was grateful for that.

I put the bag on the counter and climbed up on the stool next to Gus. Jack took the stool on the other side of me.

"Ya'll eatin'?" Sarge asked.

I glanced at Jack and he bobbed his head from side to side. "I could eat."

"Sure. I'll take the special," I said, pointing to the board. Schnitzel and butternut squash fries.

"Make it two," Jack said.

"Wine?" Sarge asked.

"God, yes," I said.

"You got anything stronger?" Jack asked.

Sarge scowled. "Yeah, but I can't sell it to you."

Jack blinked at him for a few seconds, then asked. "Can you...*give* it to me?"

Without saying anything, Sarge went into the kitchen and came back with a coffee cup. He set it in front of Jack and said, "On the house."

Jack knocked back the entire cup. When he set it back down on the counter, I picked it up and sniffed at it. The unmistakable aroma of sour mash burned my sinuses. "Now... I'll have some wine," Jack said. "Thank you."

"Hope you're not driving," Gus said. "I'm just saying..."

"He's got a reason," I said. "We think we were being followed."

"Here?" Gus asked.

"Yeah," I said. I filled him in on our journey from the clinic, as well as our divergent readings of the first three letters of the license plate.

"What kind of car was it?" Gus asked.

"I don't know. It was black. A four-door, I think," I said.

"It was a BMW 3 Series Sports Sedan," Jack said, "with custom rims."

"Check you out," I said. "So manly."

Jack ignored my jibe. Gus had pulled a moleskine from his pocket and was jotting down notes. "I'll run some options, see what we get," he said.

"There's more," I said. I placed the paper bag in front of Gus.

"What's that?" he asked.

"Dog poop," I said.

Gus blinked. Then he frowned. Then he turned to me, wordlessly awaiting an explanation.

"Betty Swann's death wasn't an accident," I said. "And neither was her dog Anselm's."

Gus moaned and rolled his eyes. "Here we go."

"Hear me out," I said, placing a hand on his arm. He looked at my hand, and I saw him soften. In my peripheral vision, I also saw Jack fidget. Was there a part of me that enjoyed his jealousy? Oh, yes. "We went to the dog show in San Diego to take possession of Abelard, Betty's other dog."

"By what authority?" Gus asked.

"By authority of her sister's ownership," I said.

"Oh. The next-of-kin?"

"Yes," I said. "He was being kept—and shown—by Austin Teal."

"Okay. And?"

"And Abelard pooped this." I pointed to the bag.

"I hope ya'll don't mind me asking," Sarge said, his hands on his hips. "But why did you bring a bag of dog poop into my restaurant?"

"It's worse than that," I said. "It might contain a biochemical agent."

"Sweet Jesus," Sarge said.

Gus sighed. "This is where I wake up and think, 'Oh, thank God it was all just a bad dream.'"

"We collected the specimen straight from the dog's anus, and it hasn't left our possession," I said. "We collected it because it was…unusual. I examined it at the clinic earlier tonight. It isn't actually feces, it's a condom filled with a white powder. I don't have the equipment to analyze it."

"Oh, I see. But I do." Gus said, staring at the bag.

"Yeah," I said. "And whatever it is, it's probably not on the up-and-up, so bringing it straight to you seemed like the prudent thing."

Gus' elbows were on the counter, and he held his head in his hands. "Oh, I hate to say this, but you did the right thing."

"You're a sweetheart," I said, instantly wondering if I'd gone too far.

Gus gave me the side-eye, which confirmed it. I wasn't interested in him, but I *was* playing him, and he knew it. I felt ashamed of myself, but I didn't let it show.

"Oh, and whatever it is, it's likely to be international," I said. "Just before the San Diego show, Teal was showing Abelard in Mexico—at the show in Mexicali."

"Well, that's good news, in a way," Gus said. "The sheriff will care a lot less if the Feds are picking up the tab. I'll get this to the FBI lab in Sacramento tomorrow."

I squeezed his bicep. "Thanks, Gus."

A bell dinged and Sarge turned to the high window into the kitchen. He retrieved two plates from the under the warming lamps and turned back toward us. "If you'll get the poop off the counter, I'll serve you your dinner," he said.

"That's my cue, I guess," Gus said, getting up.

"You don't need to go," I said.

"I've finished my dinner and my coffee. Time to shuffle off to my lonely trailer to cut my toenails and watch Jeopardy." He placed a twenty on the counter. "Thanks, Sarge. And keep the change."

Sarge saluted him. Gus grabbed the paper sack and, placing his cowboy hat on his head, strode to the doorway.

"It's cruel, what you done," Sarge said to me.

I shrank, even as I unrolled my silverware from the paper napkin. "I know."

Jack was silent, nursing his wine glass, which was very nearly empty. For some reason, a part of me justified my actions by reasoning that, if I did it out in the open, and didn't pretend that I wasn't doing it, it was somehow okay. That part of me was wrong, and I knew that. I sighed.

Then I realized there was hot schnitzel underneath my nose. Sarge set a bottle of catsup within easy reach, but Jack snagged it first.

"Well, it's out of our hands now," I said. "The Feds will have it tomorrow, and whatever it is, they'll likely need to investigate it. We can relax."

Oh, how wrong I was.

thirty-one

"Keys," I said to Jack as we left Millie's.

"Wha...?"

"An hour ago you had a bourbon and two glasses of wine," I said, in a tone that brooked no argument. "You might not be over the legal limit, but you're dancing with it."

"I'm fine," he said.

"Keys," I repeated.

He sighed and dropped the fob into my hand. I hadn't driven his car before, but I didn't see anything exceptional about it. I pushed the button on the fob and slid into the driver's seat. Grumbling, Jack took shotgun.

"Are you okay?" I asked. "You're not usually in a bad mood."

Jack looked down into his lap. "I'm sorry." He sounded defeated.

"It's Gus, isn't it?" I asked.

"You were flirting with him," he asserted.

I sighed. "Not seriously."

"Enough to confuse him and me both."

It was my turn to apologize. "I'm sorry, Jack. I could give you some bullshit about how women are socialized to exert their power, but that has never felt like a fit for me. It doesn't make it right."

He nodded, still not looking up. "What are we doing here?" he asked.

"What do you mean?" I asked.

"I mean...you and me," he said.

I looked down at the pedals. We sat in silence for a couple of minutes. Finally I said, "I've been trying to figure that out myself."

"What's getting in the way?" he asked.

I felt like a giant worm in my stomach turned over. "Do you want the truth?" I asked.

"Always," he said. He looked up at me. I met his eyes briefly and looked down again.

"I'm a scientist," I said. "And you're so...religious."

"Why is that a problem?" he asked.

"You don't see it as a problem?" I asked.

"No," he said. "I trust science. This whole science-versus-religion thing is a late-nineteenth-century invention. The great scientists of the past were also sincere people of faith."

"What changed?" I asked.

"Well, that's a complicated question, but the simple answer is Darwin—also a person of faith, by the way."

"He was?"

"Well, he wasn't a Christian, but he was definitely a theist—he believed in God," Jack conceded. "Look, I don't see the Bible as a science textbook," he continued. "Or even a reliable history book. It doesn't tell us *how* God did things. It only tells us *why*."

"Even that bothers me. How can you know? What if it's just mythology?" I asked.

He shrugged. "We can't know for sure. It's why we have to use our brains, to discern what's human stuff and what's Spirit stuff. Some of it *is* mythology." He turned to face me. "Casey, I don't believe the Bible was written from God's perspective. I think it was written from a human perspective. It's the record of two peoples' understanding of their relationship with this mysterious Presence—"

"Two peoples?" I asked.

"The Old Testament contains the memories of the Jewish people; the New Testament preserves the memories of the early Christians. But it always reports those events through the lens of their own cultural biases, prejudices, and political spin. Reading the Bible faithfully also means reading it critically. We get to talk back to it. In fact, we have a responsibility to talk back to it."

"You know, when it comes to religion, you never say what I think you're going to say," I confessed.

"There's more than one way to be religious," Jack said.

I nodded. "I just...I guess I assumed you thought along the same lines as the priests and nuns I grew up with."

"I'd be grateful if you withdrew those projections and took me on my own terms," Jack said.

"That's fair," I said. "Thank you...I guess... for having the courage to say these things to me."

"See what happens when you get me liquored up?" Jack asked.

"I didn't have anything to do with that," I said.

Jack looked around. "Are you afraid of being followed again?"

"I hadn't thought of it until you said that, so...thank you for that."

"Sorry."

"I wonder…" I started. "If the person who was following us is the same person who ran Betty Swann off the road?"

"That's a scary thought," Jack said.

"It is."

"Let's just get home," he said. "The dogs will be ready for dinner."

"I'm out of clothes," I said. "Unless you want me reeking. Can we swing by the cottage and pick up some things?"

"Sure," he agreed.

I drove to the edge of the parking lot and looked both ways. From what I could see, there were no cars on either side. I pulled onto the county road and headed for the cottage.

"But if you trust science," I said. "How can you also believe in the supernatural?"

"There are things we can explain, and things we can't explain," Jack said. "It's always been that way. Do you think we're anywhere near having every scientific mystery figured out?"

"Of course not," I said.

"No. Science is the realm of what we can know. Philosophy and theology are the realms of speculation."

"You don't *know* there is a God?" I asked.

"I know for sure that when I reach out, something or someone reaches back," Jack said. "That's not speculation—"

"It's not science either," I added.

"Touché," he said. "But it is my experience, and you don't get to argue with that."

"Fair enough," I said.

"That something or someone is a mystery—a capital 'M' Mystery. But it's hard to be in relationship with a Mystery. The human brain needs to give it a face. It's how we're constructed."

"Is one face as good as another?" I asked.

"The Hindus say that there is only one God—"

"I thought they had a million gods," I objected.

He held up his hand. "The Hindus say there is only one God, but that God has a million faces. So you find the face that resonates with your heart and serve that face."

"And do you believe that too?" I asked.

"I do," he said.

"And which face resonates with your heart?"

"You have to ask?" He smiled.

"Let me guess," I said. "Jesus."

"Bingo," he said. "I am in love with Jesus."

"I'm not sure how to take that," I said.

"I'm inviting you into a threesome," he said.

I laughed out loud. "You are so, so weird."

I was so engaged in the conversation I had been driving on autopilot, but as we rounded the last corner, the shock of recognition pulled me back into the moment. I pulled into the driveway of the cottage and shut off the engine.

"Do you want me to come in?" he asked.

"Sure. Otherwise, you'll be snoring by the time I get back."

"You wound me," Jack said.

"The truth hurts," I retorted.

He slipped his arm into mine as we walked toward the cottage. Then I froze.

"What?" Jack asked. I pointed. "Oh."

Dusk was settling over the sky, but there was still enough light left to see that the red door of the cottage was slightly ajar. A stab of raw wood cut through the red paint at the rightmost edge, and a spray of splinters erupted from the doorpost at precisely the place where the deadbolt would have slid in.

"Looks like someone took a crowbar to your door," Jack said.

"It sure does," I said.

He tugged at my arm, "Back to the car. Quick. Call Gus."

I didn't need him to tell me twice. We both jogged back to his Mini Cooper, slid in, and locked our doors. "Drive," he said.

I drove. I held my phone to my face, and once I was in, I passed it to Jack. "Call."

He called. After three rings, Gus picked up. "Casey? Can't get enough of me, huh?"

"Gus, you're on speakerphone with me and Jack—"

"Oh," he said. I could almost hear him gulp.

"We're at the cottage. Someone broke in."

"Did you go in?" he asked.

"No. We hightailed it to the car. We're just doing a loop now."

"Thank God. Keep driving. I'll have the black-and-whites there pronto. I'll see you soon."

"You don't need—" I started, but he'd hung up.

"Can't get enough of him, huh?" Jack said.

"Shut up," I said.

Despite everything, he laughed. I chalked it up to the alcohol.

By the time we circled back to the cottage, the police were there. Heartened, I parked and jogged up the walkway toward the door. Jack followed, walking.

I didn't recognize the first policeman, but he saw me coming, and moved to intercept. "Are you the owner?"

"I'm the renter...the occupant," I said. I put out my hand. "Dr. Casey Gibbons."

He shook my hand, but without warmth. His name tag read *Carrol*.

"Case!" I heard Gus' voice before I saw him. He jogged to meet us at just about the time Jack caught up to me.

"Did you go in?" Gus asked.

"No," Officer Carrol and I said together.

"All clear!" another officer shouted from the front door.

I could see Gus visibly relax. He was still in his street clothes, but his service revolver was in a holster at his hip. "Wait here," he said.

I took a deep breath and let it out slowly. "Gus!" I said.

He turned.

"I need clothes. That's why we stopped by here."

"This is a crime scene now," he said. "I'm sorry, but I can't let you take anything in or out. Not until the CSU is finished— and they haven't even arrived yet. They're on the way from Auburn." He turned again and entered the cottage.

"Damn," I breathed.

Jack's arm squeezed my shoulder. "It's okay. We'll go by the Goodwill tomorrow. You can wear some of my clothes tonight while we wash what you've got."

I nodded. Only Stacy would care that I wore the same clothes three days in a row, and I decided not to care that she cared. At least my laptop was in the car. Then I felt a moment of panic. I rushed toward the front door and called out, "Gus, I only really have one thing of value—the ashes of my last dog, Penny. They should be in a pine box on the mantle over the fire. Will you check?"

"Sure. Wait here." I watched as Gus went in. Jack slipped his hand over mine and squeezed. I buried my face in his shoulder. I felt numb.

After about five minutes, Gus exited, his face grim. I stepped way from Jack, nearly standing on tiptoe in my anxiety. Gus moved toward us slowly, almost as if buying himself time to decide what he was going to say to me.

"Just spill it," I said, when he was in easy earshot.

He looked down and shook his head. Then he took off his cowboy hat and ran his fingers through his hair.

"Gus—what?" I demanded.

"Your house is messed up pretty good," he said. "But the ashes are still there. The box had been knocked to the floor, but it isn't broken."

"Thank God." I felt a rush of relief. "What were they looking for?" I asked.

"I don't think they were looking for anything," he said. "I think they were just busting stuff up."

"Busting stuff—what stuff?"

"Furniture, books—"

"Jesus!" I swore.

"They tried to make it look like they were looking for something, but they weren't very thorough. It looks like they were just going for dramatic effect."

I shook my head, my fists balling into tight pockets of lightning. Jack tried to squeeze my shoulders again, but I shrugged him off. I was too angry for comfort.

Gus looked at his shoes. "And...uh...they left this." He handed me his phone. I tried to take it, but my hands were shaking. Jack, steadied by the bourbon no doubt, held it instead. It was a photo of my bedroom wall. Written in red, splotchy block letters was, "BITCHES GET PUT DOWN."

"The passive mood suggests a threat," Jack noted.

"Gee, d'you think?" I snapped. Then I screamed. I had tried to contain my rage and frustration, but I failed. I swung my fists and very nearly connected with Jack's nose. He stepped back, eyes wide. All the cops froze and turned toward me.

"I'm sorry, Case," Gus said. "I really am. It's...it's just a good thing you weren't there. Or Scout."

I bit my lip as hot tears forced their way out of my eyes.

Gus sidled up to me, and in a soft voice, he said, "Go get some rest, Casey. I'll handle things here. We'll put a padlock on the door. I'll bring you the key. Just...go have a drink, or a bath.

Go hug your dog. Take care of yourself. There's nothing more you can do tonight."

He was right, dammit. I knew he was right. But I wanted to hurt someone—or something. I wanted to break boards with my bare hands or smash glass against a wall or take a sledge-hammer to someone's head.

"Gus is right," Jack said, not getting too close. I felt a twinge of guilt. "Let's go to my place. We can swing by the clinic and pick up your car on the way. I'm fine to drive now. C'mon."

He turned and walked back to the car. I half expected Gus to challenge him, but he didn't. Everyone was looking at me. I sighed, crossed my arms, and stormed after Jack, looking and feeling like a petulant teenager who wasn't getting her way.

But I would.

thirty-two

The next morning, I pulled into the parking lot of the clinic and just sat there, engine off. My chest hurt and I was having trouble getting a full breath—classic signs of anxiety. I forced myself to breathe deeply. Then I tried to think of nothing—rather than the endless, obsessive mental rehearsals of the night before. That was a royal failure. I remember someone saying, "Try not to think of a white elephant." What happens? A white elephant is *all* you can think about.

Get a grip, Case, the voice in my head ordered. It occurred to me that being at work might actually help distract me from my white elephant obsessions and might even help ground me. "Good Lord, I'm starting to sound like Jack."

I got out of the car and shut the door. I instantly surveilled the area, looking for some sign—any sign—of danger. I was met with nothing but the empty county road and a light breeze. *Breathe*, the voice advised me. I went in through the service entrance at the side of the building.

I felt Stacy's eyes on me—peering at me from over her cat's-eye glasses. Did she notice that I was wearing yesterday's clothes? Of course she did. I ignored the stare and issued a general greeting. "Morning."

"G'morning, Doctor Casey," Ginny, one of our assistants said from behind the desk. Ginny was a single mother. I don't know how she survived on what we paid her, but she never complained.

Once in back, Ellie came up behind me and whispered. "Did you find out what was in the condom?"

"No, not yet," I said. "It's with the FBI."

"The FBI?" she squealed. She clamped her hands over her mouth, trying to quell her response. "Sorry. That's so exciting."

I didn't respond. I flipped through the mail in my in-box and threw every single piece of it away except for a scrip request. That I put in the pocket of my lab coat.

"Did your friend surprise you?" Ellie asked.

I stopped. I turned to face her. "Friend?"

"Yeah. Handsome fella. Chin like an anvil."

I blinked. I only knew one person who fit that description.

Ella continued. "Old school chum of yours? Didn't say what school. He seemed at ease around animals, so I assumed veterinary college. You went to Davis, right?"

I continued to blink.

"Casey, what's wrong?"

"What did this...friend...want?"

"He...uh...he wanted to surprise you. To drop in and say hi." I watched her deflate. "Did I do something wrong?"

"Ellie, did you give him my address?" I asked.

"Uh...yeah. I didn't see how it could hurt. He said he was—"

"A friend. I know. You said." Through clenched teeth, I bit back on my anger. Ellie was young, she was excitable. She was a good friend, but she didn't always have the best judgement. "Listen, Ellie, last night someone trashed my cottage."

"What do you mean, trashed?" I watched the color drain from her face.

"I mean, they busted through my front door with a crowbar, smashed everything smashable inside, and spray painted 'Bitches get put down' on my bedroom wall."

Her eyes grew as big as Oreos and her hand covered her open mouth. "Oh my God!"

I met her eyes and held them. I was not happy. And she got that.

"Oh my God, Casey," she repeated. "I'm so sorry. I thought —I never would have—oh my God!"

Then it was as if someone had pulled the rug out from under her. Her eyes rolled back into her head and she went down, fast and hard. I dove for the floor and succeeded in getting my hand between her head and the floor. I winced with the impact, and my hand instantly began to throb. "Stacy!" I yelled.

A moment later, Stacy appeared around the corner. She froze when she saw us both on the floor. "Call an ambulance!" I yelled. She hesitated. "Now!" She dove for the phone.

I had had enough of emergency vehicles, but this wasn't about me. The paramedics were quick, and in what seemed like mere minutes, Ellie had been loaded onto a gurney and was on her way to Sierra Nevada Memorial.

"I should go to the hospital," I said to Stacy.

She handed me a manila folder. "You should see your next client. Exam Room Four."

"But—"

"I'll call her family. You do your job."

If I had had x-ray eyes like Superman, there would be two smoking holes in Stacy's skull. Since I was a mere mortal, I snatched up the folder and headed to Four. No doubt Ellie would still be at the hospital when I got off work. I'd see her then.

I didn't even look at the folder—I just headed for Room Four on autopilot. My head was spinning. It stopped abruptly when I opened the door.

Massaman was sitting in one of the two chairs, his creepy hairless cat on his lap.

"Dr. Gibbons—or can I call you Casey, now that we are friends?"

Massaman was an enormous man. His Thai features communicated an ironic serenity given that he was the most dangerous mob-connected criminal I had ever met—that I know of. Shelley had borrowed $20,000 from him before she was murdered, and now I—or rather, the clinic—was paying it off, to the tune of $500 per month.

"I wasn't aware that we were friends," I said, trying to regain my equilibrium.

"Well, we are not enemies, are we?" he asked.

"I hope not...no," I said. "You've been very fair."

"And you have been most reliable in your payments. As a businessman, that is all I could ask for." He gave me a condescending smile.

"I take it you're not really here because Jok needs a checkup," I said, sitting in the other chair.

"That would be correct."

"So...to what do I owe the pleasure?"

"Please assure me that there are no recording devices employed in this room," Massaman said.

I frowned. "No. No, there aren't any devices."

"Good...because I would hate for anything that I have to say to you to be...repeatable in any form."

I shook my head. "We have complete privacy here. You

have my word." I also knew that he would probably slit my throat if I was lying.

"Good. I do the...assorted odd job...for some very powerful and influential people."

I nodded. That could mean almost anything, but I think I understood *exactly* what he meant.

"Last week I was hired to watch someone."

"Uh...who?"

"This man." He pulled his phone out of his pocket and held it up. I leaned in and found myself looking directly at Austin Teal.

"I know him," I said, my voice dripping with poison.

"Yesterday, I followed him to a cute little cottage out on Parsons Road."

I lived on Parsons Road. I bolted up in my seat. I probably gained two inches, and I hadn't even been slouching before. "Yeah?"

He flipped to another picture. It was unmistakably Teal, with a crowbar, working on my front door.

"That's valuable evidence," I said.

"No, it isn't." He put the phone back in his pocket. "It is work product, and it does not belong to you...or to me. It belongs solely to my client."

I felt lightheaded and realized I was hyperventilating. I forced myself to breathe slower. "Mr. Massaman, why are you here?"

He gave me that self-satisfied smile again. "I am not an honest man, Doctor. But I like people who pay their debts. If they die, it is harder to collect."

He winked, which was creepy. There were a lot of unspoken messages in that statement, some about Shelley, some about me. He leaned in and whispered. "I am a business-man. It does not serve me to lose income streams."

So that's what I am, I thought. *I'm an income stream. Good to know.*

"And besides that," he said, leaning back and speaking normally again. "I like your style, Dr. Casey. You have..." he drew his lips back and showed me his impossibly white teeth. "...pluck."

He was right about that. I have pluck in spades. I have a freaking truckful of pluck, sometimes to my detriment.

"Are you here to warn me?" I said. "Because I've already seen the cottage."

"I am relieved to see you weren't hurt." He sounded sincere.

"I was...staying with a friend," I said.

"Lucky friend."

Jack hadn't gotten lucky yet, but Massaman didn't need to know that. I struggled with how much to tell Massaman. I decided that the enemy of my enemy was my friend. "I think Teal is using dogs to smuggle...something...across the Mexican border into the US. He's making them swallow condoms filled with...I don't know what—poison, drugs, something. Then they're pooping it out on this side of the border. I'm onto him... and he knows it."

"Ah...that makes a lot of sense." I could see his eyes moving back and forth as he thought. "The people I work for...they have, let us say, *interests* in Mexico."

"And they are paying you to watch Teal because...?"

He chuckled. "Because they are businessmen, too. And they don't like to lose income streams any more than I do."

I nodded. "I snatched one of Teal's dogs and sent the condom out for testing—"

"Which means Mr. Teal is down several thousand dollars' worth of product," Massaman said slowly, pointing at me.

"And one reliable mule," I finished.

"Exactly. A *valuable* mule."

I was suddenly terrified that Teal would try to steal Abelard back. I kicked myself for not bringing him to work. I could have put him in the kennel while I was working. I vowed that tomorrow I would.

Without warning, Massaman stood, cradling Jok in his left arm and absent-mindedly stroking the cat's head with his free hand. "It is always a pleasure, Dr. Casey."

I nodded, still trying to take it all in. Massaman opened the door to the waiting room, but then closed it again. He dug a card out of his pocket and handed it to me. There was no name on the card, nothing but a phone number. "In case you need me," he said. "Oh, and I hope you'll take comfort in this and not...take it the wrong way, but...I am watching."

thirty-three

I hadn't made a single note in Jok's file—there was no reason to. I moved to place the untouched file on Stacy's desk, but dropped it, spilling its contents. I expected Stacy to yell at me, or at least to glower, but instead she raised one eyebrow and said, "You look rattled."

I looked down. Busted. "I am," I said.

"Are those the same clothes you were wearing yesterday?" she asked.

So busted. "They are. I—"

"I heard about what happened to your house," she interrupted. "I'm so sorry, Doctor."

I looked at her face and saw that she was sincere. She even looked a little bit worried about me.

"Thank you," I said. I shifted from one foot to another. Then I turned back to the rack where Stacy put our "in play" files. "I don't see a file for the next client."

"Mrs. Martin cancelled," Stacy said. "Go and get yourself together."

I bristled a bit at her tone, but I was too grateful for the extra time to ruin it with an unnecessary confrontation. I nodded and headed for the break room. To my dismay, Ajeet was there, putting teaspoon after teaspoon of sugar into his chai.

"Want some tea with that sugar?" I asked. I sat down heavily.

He looked up at me but didn't say anything. He was still angry. But I was drama-ed out. There was so much else going on that Ajeet's anger didn't even register. That was probably a mistake, but that's the way it was.

"I heard about your cottage," Ajeet said. "I'm sorry."

"Thanks," I said. "They busted a lot of stuff up. At least they didn't take—or break—the ashes."

"Ashes?" he asked.

"Of my Boxer Peggy," I said.

"Ah." He nodded sadly.

"I'm sorry I used you," I said. I hadn't planned on saying it. It just fell out of my lips unbidden. I instantly stiffened.

"I know you are sorry," he said. "But that doesn't excuse what you did."

I looked down. "No, it doesn't."

He rose. "If you'll excuse me, I have a box of homeopathic preparations to put away."

I nodded. When he was out of the room, I sighed. I really did like Ajeet; I felt the rupture in our still-young relationship keenly. His methods were eccentric, but I had to admit he got great results, and it was abundantly clear how much he cared. I felt a wave of shame wash through me and hugged myself.

My phone buzzed. I whipped it out and saw that I had a message from Gus. "FBI wants a meeting at noon. Sheriff's Office. Can U B there?"

"Yes," I typed and put my phone away. Then I texted Jack

and asked him to meet me there. A moment later my phone buzzed again. I was relieved to see that he could.

I had only one client remaining before lunch. An Alaskan Malamute had an infected anal sac. It was too painful to express it in the regular fashion, so I had to infuse it with an antibiotic/steroid ointment. We were finally successful, but when the sac finally gave up its treasure, the effluvia that resulted shot a full four feet, spraying the wall. *Good thing I'm skipping lunch,* I thought.

Stacy tried to catch my attention on my way out the door, but I couldn't let her distract me. If I left immediately, I'd just make it to Utah City in time for the meeting.

I usually listen to the Sacramento NPR affiliate in the car, but today I turned the radio off as I drove. The silence was delicious. I decided I needed more silence in my life. *Do I need more silence? Or less craziness?* the voice in my head wondered. *Why choose?* I answered back.

When I got to the Sheriff's Office, Jack was already there, waiting in the lobby. I checked in at the desk and sat next to him, dropping into my seat like a bag of rocks.

"Tough day?" Jack asked.

"My colleague hates me. And then anal sacks."

Jack looked away and nodded. "I think I can fill in the blanks."

He reached for my hand. I took it, squeezed it, let it go.

A door opened at the far side of the lobby, and Gus poked his head in. He brightened when he saw us. "They're ready for you now."

We rose and followed him—through the door and down the hall. "Oh, Case, here's the key to the padlock." He fished a key from his uniform khakis and handed it to me. "Didn't want you to think the cottage was open to the world."

"Thank you, Gus," I said, pocketing the key.

Gus led us to a glass-walled conference room. Even before we entered, I could see the County Sheriff and two black-suited agents, a man and a woman. The woman was soft, short, and curvy. She wore her thick red hair in a bob. The man was her polar opposite—tall, bald, and thin as a pipe cleaner.

They both stood as we entered. Gus waved us over to two chairs on the far side of a large table that dominated the room. We sat directly opposite the agents. Gus cleared his throat. "Uh, Dr. Casey Gibbons and Fr. Jack Mornington, this is our County Sheriff, Sandall Pruitt."

The Sheriff—who did not rise to meet us—nodded in our direction. Jack waved nervously at him.

Gus continued, "And this is Special Agent Tammy Knight and Special Agent Thomas Kincaid."

Jack piped up, "As in Thomas Kincaid™, painter of light?"

Special Agent Kincaid narrowed his eyes at him and frowned.

"So no relation then?" Jack asked.

Kincaid turned toward the Sheriff. "I'm not sure why we need the priest."

"That's a common opinion these days," Jack said.

I raised one eyebrow. "We need him because he was there. He's a material witness to a crime."

"As are you," Kincaid said.

"I didn't see the condom emerge from the dog's bunghole," I said. "Jack did."

"It's a chain-of-custody thing, Tom," Special Agent Knight said, leaning slightly toward her partner.

"I guess," he said.

"Now, I'm so glad you're here." Knight beamed a broad, seemingly sincere smile at us. She had on an almost neon lipstick, and her southern accent sounded adorable to my ears.

"Thank you for taking time out of your busy day to talk with us. We're ever so grateful to you."

Special Agent Kincaid folded his hands in front of him and scowled. "We brought cookies."

He stared at us. We stared at him. Several moments of silence passed. Special Agent Knight slapped his arm and said, "Don't keep us in suspense, Tom. Just put out the damn cookies."

Without taking his eyes off us, Kincaid reached down into the empty chair next to him and lifted a plate covered with tin foil. He placed the plate on the table within our reach and unwrapped the foil as if he were defusing a bomb. He carefully folded it and placed the resulting shiny rectangle in his shirt pocket. His solemn gaze never once left our faces.

"These are a family specialty," Agent Knight said. "Burnt-sugar cookies with butterscotch chips. I made them myself, just last night. Thought it might help us get off on the right foot."

Jack didn't need to be asked twice. He snatched a cookie and took a bite. "That's amazing!"

"Thank you, Father. That means so much to my heart." She leaned back in her seat and patted her chest, looking momentarily as if she might cry.

"Uh...if you all don't mind, I have a busy morning," Sheriff Pruitt said.

"Oh, of course, darlin'," Agent Knight said, giving him a little wave. She turned to Jack and me. "I just want to make sure we got our p's and q's jotted and tittled, here, so why don't you tell us the whole story, from your perspective?" She pressed a button on her phone. "Ya'll don't mind if we're recording this, do you?"

"I don't mind," I said. I began with the dog show where

Jack and I watched Anselm die. I ended with the story of us giving the paper sack with the condom in it to Gus at Millie's Diner.

"That was a lovely story," she smiled sweetly at me, looking for all the world like a great aunt I wanted desperately to please. "And well told. You deserve a cookie."

A very young part of myself basked in this weird praise and believed that yes, yes indeed, I did deserve a cookie. As if watching myself from afar, I took one.

"And you, Father Mornington," Knight said, turning to Jack. "Do you concur with Dr. Gibbon's testimony?"

"I do, in every detail. Although, as Casey said, she didn't see the poop actually coming out of Abelard's butt. I did." Jack looked entirely too pleased with himself. Who was this woman, I wondered, and what kind of spell was she casting? She made me feel very uncomfortable, yet at the same time I desperately wanted to show her the picture I'd made gluing macaroni to some construction paper.

"That's just fine," she said, making a note. "Is there anything else you'd like to tell us?" She looked up at me, specifically, her eyes holding mine. I thought about Massaman's photo showing Teal breaking into my cottage. But bringing Massaman into this seemed like a betrayal of trust. "I...no... nothing further."

"Well, someone vandalized your house, I understand," Agent Knight said, not quite a question.

"Yes, they did. I believe it was Austin Teal."

"But you don't know that for sure," Agent Knight said, still not quite a question.

I did know it for sure. But I couldn't tell her that. "Who else could it be?"

"It does seem likely to have been Teal," Agent Kincaid asserted, his face completely void of emotion.

"Now, Tom, what have I told you about rushing to hasty judgments?" Knight whispered in Kincaid's direction. Kincaid said nothing. His face was stone.

"Did you test the sample?" I asked.

"We did," Kincaid said.

"Twice," added Knight. She leaned down and rummaged in something on the floor, a briefcase, I surmised. She pulled up a manila folder, set it down in front of her, and opened it to reveal a meager four sheets of paper. She read from the top sheet. "It contained Fentanyl, in a very, very concentrated form," she poured over a couple of the other pages. "My, my— very dangerous." She shut the folder again and beamed up at me. "You both done so good, bringing this to us."

"Can I have another cookie?" Jack asked.

"You deserve two," Knight said, winking at him.

"What now?" I asked, acutely conscious of the time and of the fact that I had a kitten with an abscess to lance in less than an hour. Joy.

"Clearly, someone—whether it is Austin Teal or someone else—means you no good," Knight said, turning to me.

"Clearly," I agreed.

"So...we'd like to take advantage of that, to see if we can catch...whoever it is."

I blinked. Then I looked over at Jack. He was blinking. I turned back to Knight. "Go on," I prompted.

She leaned down, placing her elbows on the table in front of her, and sliding a few inches toward us. Then she lowered her head and spoke in a low voice, not quite whispering. "We want you to help us catch him—assuming it's a 'him,'" she said.

"Okay," I agreed. "How would I do that?"

"We just want you to go home," she said, smiling.

"Home...to the cottage?" I asked.

She nodded. "Just make it look normal. Take your duffle bag or whatever—and your dog—and just go home."

"My home isn't fit to live in," I said.

"So you have a project when you get there," she said.

I had to admit that going home and asserting order on the mess that had been wrecked on my space sounding amazingly appealing. In fact, I was dying to get my hands on the place—to make it mine again.

"Okay, so if I go home, what do you do?" I asked.

"We lie in wait."

"A stakeout?" Jack asked.

"Exactly," Kincaid said. "We catch him in the act."

For a few moments, no one said anything. Then Jack said, "Absolutely not. It's too dangerous."

I turned on him. "Jack," I said softly, "It's not your decision."

"I have an opinion, and I have a right to express it," he said.

"Then express it as an opinion," I said, "Not a *fait accompli*."

His shoulders sagged. "I'm sorry," he said. "I just...I'm scared."

I reached over and put my hand on top of his. "I know. So am I. But I want to take this risk."

I turned back to Knight. "But I want to leave Scout at Jack's."

She shook her head. "He knows you're a dog person. If you go there without your dog, he'll know something is up."

"I'm willing to put myself in danger, but not her," I said.

"There won't be any danger," Kincaid said, his voice raspy and testy.

Knight gave him the eye, but then said, "Tom's right. We'll nab him—or whoever it is—before he even gets to your house."

"How will you go undetected?" Jack asked.

"We have our ways," Kincaid said, as if that was an answer.

"I'll just bet you do," Jack said, his eyes narrowing.

"What do you say, Dr. Gibbons? Will you help us?" Knight asked, in a drawl so sweet it reminded me of peach tea.

"I'm in," I said.

thirty-four

I 'm not sure how it happened, but somehow, over the past several days of staying with Jack, I had amassed enough *stuff* to need a box. I carried the box to my car and then returned to the gloomy mock-Tudor to get Scout. Tripod could tell something was up—he was whining. He hadn't been with Jack long, but he was already clued in to his master's anxiety. I clipped Scout's leash to her collar, and Jack walked with me to the door. "You don't have to do this," he said.

"I know," I said. "But...a part of me needs to."

He nodded. He knew his protest was a lost cause, and he didn't belabor it. He already knew me pretty well, it seemed. He did, however, try a different tack. "I'd feel a lot better if I were coming with you."

I didn't need to explain all the reasons that wasn't a good idea. Instead, I faced him and, going up on tiptoe, planted a lingering kiss on his fabulous lips. I felt a surge of oxytocin and savored it.

The chemistry of love.

I turned, and Scout went out ahead of me, only stopped short by the leash. I waved over my shoulder, not daring to look back. I didn't want to see his face—sad, worried, troubled...

I don't remember the car ride over. I do remember that sometime during the drive, my phone rang. I pressed the button on the console to take it over my car's speakers. "Dr. Gibbons here," I said.

"Dr. Gibbons, bless your heart," Special Agent Knight's voice crackled a bit as I passed under high-tension wires. "We have you on the move. You goin' home, darlin'?"

"I'm about halfway there," I said.

"That's just fine. I just wanted you to know that everything —and everyone—is in place. Now...you and your pretty little dog don't need to worry 'bout a bloomin' thing, ya' hear me? We *got this*, girlfriend."

I winced at the agent's unearned intimacies, but I didn't object aloud. "Good to know. Thank you, Agent Knight."

"That's *Special* Agent Knight," she corrected me, "because we all need remindin' that we're special. But you can call me Tammy, alright, sweetheart? Or Tams if you're a little tipsy. I won't mind."

"Uh...okay...Tammy. Thank you."

"The next time you see me, you won't have a thing to worry about from Mr. Teal."

"You sound pretty sure," I said.

"I got a feelin' about things," she said. "Ain't been wrong yet."

"A feeling..." I repeated. I was a scientist. I *had* feelings, but I didn't tend to trust them. If my feelings were a teenager, I would not give them the keys to my car. I wasn't sure how I felt about having Tammy Knight's feelings in the driver's seat. Oh wait—yes I did....I did not like it one bit. "I hope you're right," I said, with more diplomacy than my delinquent feelings were really comfortable with.

"You just go in there like it's any other day after work. You got your new broom and mop?"

"My old broom and mop are just fine. He didn't bust up my cleaning supplies."

"Might help you feel like you're making a fresh start, having a new broom and mop—"

"Tammy?" I interrupted.

"Yes, darlin'?"

"A girl has a right to choose her own cleaning supplies."

"Well, bless your heart. I see your point, and I appreciate you setting clear and appropriate boundaries. You are a very, *very* good girl."

If Special Agent Knight were in the passenger seat I would have slugged her, and she would have seen just what a good girl I actually was—good with my fists. "Anything else?" I asked.

"Nope, that's it for us. Just relax and try to enjoy puttin' your house in order."

I was getting the feeling that, for all her praline sweetness, Tammy was a bit of a control freak. I hoped she didn't have kids, because...I shuddered to think.

"Now don't worry about a thing. 'Bye, darlin'." The connection clicked off.

"Holy crap, lady," I said. Scout was staring at me from the passenger seat, her big brown eyes unwavering, even as her body jostled and bounced from the potholes in the county road.

"Stop looking at me like that. She's not *that* nice a lady."

Scout kept staring.

"Boy, does she have you fooled," I said.

And then I was turning off the road into my driveway. I

coasted to a stop and looked. I couldn't see any cars—FBI or otherwise. Everything looked as quiet and serene as it ever had. *This is my home*, the voice in my head reminded me. For good or ill, this was where I belonged...where I most longed to be. "Let's do this," I said to Scout. I leaned over and unclipped her leash. There was no need for it here. Scout knew better than to wander onto the road.

We walked together toward the cottage, Scout heeling without being told to. Probably she was sensing something I couldn't—and most likely it was just my own anxiety. True to Gus' word, the police had rigged up a padlock. I pulled the key Gus had given me from my pocket and inserted it. The padlock sprang open, and I swung the door in.

Scout sprang inside and I followed. I turned on the lights, as dusk was falling fast. The place smelled of rot, but I didn't know why. Scout's nose was on the carpet, buzzing around the wrecked living room, gathering information I would have given my eyeteeth to know.

I realized I'd left the box in the car, and I went back out to retrieve it. Still, I saw nothing out of the ordinary. If the FBI were around, they were doing a very good job of hiding it. I wasn't sure how I felt about that.

Back inside, I started asserting order, starting with the living room. I carried the ruined plants out the back door and set them on the ground—I'd deal with them later. I turned a slashed couch cushion upside down to hide the violation. The glass top of the coffee table had been smashed. Fortunately, the shattered glass seemed to be mostly contained by the bottom of the table frame. I retrieved the kitchen trash can and gingerly disposed of the largest pieces. Then I swept up the rest.

I was relieved to see that Scout had taken refuge amongst the chaos on her dog bed—which Teal had left blessedly unmolested. The last thing I needed was her getting a sliver of glass in her paw. I carried the carcass of the coffee table out the front door and piled it near the trash cans. Then I retrieved my antique hope chest from the bedroom and, grunting, set it in front of the couch. "Casey, use your coasters," I admonished myself, sounding eerily like my mother.

Groaning, I got to my feet and carried the trash can, broom, and dustpan into the kitchen, where new horrors awaited. Feces had been smeared on the floor and the walls—whether human or animal, I had no way to tell, not at home anyway. I had always hated the high-gloss paint on the kitchen walls, but today I was glad of it. Never saw that coming.

After the feces, I swept up the glass from the broken cupboard window. Teal might have emptied my set of dishes and smashed those, too, but he hadn't. "Thank God for small favors," I muttered.

I realized my cleanup job wasn't a one-evening affair. I told myself this was a first pass, just getting the worst of it. That helped me relax a little.

Next, I went into the bedroom and put my hands on my hips, looking at the spray-painted threat about bitches being put down. I didn't have anything to paint over it. "Cover it another way," I said out loud. I went to my linen closet and rummaged around. A sheet? No. I went back out to the living room and opened the antique hope chest. Inside, among a stack of musty-smelling keepsakes, I found a beautiful afghan my aunt Priya had given me a couple of years ago. I snagged a couple of pushpins from the junk drawer in the kitchen and, snatching up a chair, carried it to the bedroom.

Balancing on the chair, I hung the afghan on the wall with the pushpins so that it covered the graffiti. The afghan was a lovely work of art, and I wondered why I hadn't hung it up years earlier. It did the job handily.

I had just stepped down from the chair when I heard a loud thump from the back of the house. I froze. Scout started barking, and I heard the jingle of her tags as she raced toward the sound. "Scout!" I yelled. "Come!" Her tags grew quieter, then jingly again and louder as she approached. I was relieved to hear the clackety-clackety of her nails on the hardwood floor as she came down the hall. "Come," I said again, not as loud. As soon as she reached me, I knelt and hugged her.

"Stay with me," I commanded, even though that was not a command she knew. I cast about for some sort of weapon, but there was nothing to hand in the bedroom. I had a hammer in the junk drawer. That would have to do.

Crouching, I kept one hand on Scout's collar, and we moved quickly and silently through the living room to the kitchen. I jerked open the drawer and snatched up the hammer. Then I turned to Scout. "Stay," I said. She whined. There was excitement afoot, and I was shutting her out of it. I wish I could have explained. But I couldn't. I pointed at her for emphasis. "Stay," I said again.

She sat, and I turned toward the rear of the cottage. With slow movements, I approached the back door. I weighed the hammer in my hand, acquainting myself with its feel and heft. My ears strained for any further sound, but I heard none. I paused by the back door. It was locked. I looked outside, but it was dark. I saw nothing. I switched on the outside light and saw little more.

I don't know what possessed me, but for some reason, I unlocked the door and stepped out, listening for a sound—any sound—that might be out of the ordinary. My foot met with something bumpy and soft. I leaped back and looked down. I had stepped on a dead bird.

Then it twitched. I knelt and examined it in the dim light. I hadn't stepped on it hard—as soon as I had detected something off, I'd shifted my weight to my other foot. Squinting, I saw that it was a sparrow. Its beak was broken, along with its left wing, jutting out at an impossible, unnatural angle.

Then I realized what had happened. The sparrow had flown into the glass of the back door window—that had been the thump I had heard. Did birds fly at night? I wondered. Well, this one had. I sighed. The poor thing was suffering, and there was no way it would survive on its own. I knew I could walk out to the car and get my medical bag. I could take it to the bird rescue—the little guy was a bit afield of my particular expertise. But I knew the bird rescue didn't take common birds like sparrows. On the other hand, I could euthanize the little guy. It wouldn't take much. But I was rattled and didn't much care for the idea of going out to the car to fetch my bag. On the other hand, I did have this hammer...

In the end, I decided to wring its neck. I had practiced the technique on chickens while I was in vet school. The bodies of chickens have heft, and you can spin them—which breaks their necks pretty efficiently. But a sparrow is too light, it won't spin. I dropped the hammer and took the bird up in both hands. With a quick twist, I felt the little neck snap, and I tossed its carcass out into the dark. I didn't even hear it land.

As simple as it was to dispatch the sparrow, it was still a grisly affair. It did nothing to quiet my jangly nerves. I had no sooner shut the door again when my phone rang. I literally jumped several inches off the ground at the sound of it.

"Jesus," I swore, and snatched it from my pocket. I didn't recognize the number. Dreading whatever mysterious voice might emerge from the phone, and whatever threats it might bring with it, I hit the green button to accept the call. "Hello?" I asked. My voice was wavering, reedy.

"Dr. Gibbons, you can relax now," Agent Knight's annoyingly cheerful voice informed me. "We got him."

thirty-five

"Are you sure?" I asked. "You really have him?"

"Sure as rain on game day, darlin'," Agent Knight assured me. "We're going to take him into Sacramento now and book him. You can relax and maybe even enjoy your evening. How does that sound?"

"I'd say it sounds pretty darn good." I said. That was when I noticed my hands were trembling. They also had bird blood on them from the sparrow's injured beak. I hit the button for speakerphone, put the phone down, and washed my hands.

"I'll be in touch soon. Ya'll have a nice night, y'hear?"

"Yes, and..." I swallowed as relief, gratitude, and several other unidentified, unexpected emotions rolled through me. "Tammy...thank you."

"Bless your heart, you remembered my name! You just made my evenin'. 'Night." She hung up.

I turned to face my dog. Her eyes were on my face—and I may be projecting here—but she seemed to be smiling. "I'll bet you're hungry," I said. The stub of her tail began to twitch, which was adorable. "But first...this is a job for whisky." I pulled a tumbler from the cupboard and grabbed a bottle of single malt from the counter. I thanked Jack's Jesus that it hadn't been smashed and poured myself a finger. I knocked it back and then poured two more. Those I would sip.

I fed Scout, and as she ate, I sat at the kitchen table and watched her, admiring her strength, her beauty. Her black-and-gold stripes seemed more pronounced in the yellow light of the kitchen. The gold in her coat reminded me of what was truly valuable, and just how fortunate I was.

"Here's to you, my little love," I said, raising my glass to her. She was oblivious, of course, licking away at her now-empty bowl. I thought about asking Jack to come over. "A night like this a fella could get lucky," I said out loud. Plus, I would be good and tipsy by the time he got here, which translates into "good and horny" for me. I decided that, while I still had a lingering grip on good judgment, I probably shouldn't push it. But Jack did need to know what had happened. I reached for my phone.

Then I heard another thud, again at the back door. This one was louder. It sounded more solid. "What the—" I began, but before I could get out of my chair, the door swung open, and Austin Teal stepped in.

He was dressed in black from head-to-foot. And he was holding my hammer in his right hand. The hammer I'd dropped outside when I picked up the sparrow. I instantly pieced together what had happened—he'd snuck up on my back door, and not seeing the hammer, had accidentally kicked it into the wood of the door. That was the thud. At that point, he knew the game was up. So he picked up the hammer—my only weapon—and came into the house.

Scout launched into a long string of alarmed, aggressive

barking. "Scout, to me," I said. Not pausing in her vocal protest, she did at least obey.

I put my hands behind me and backed up to the kitchen counter. With my fingers, I caught the edge of my utensil drawer and stepped toward Teal again, drawing it open behind me. "What do you want?" I asked.

"Only what's mine," he said. Every time I had seen Teal, he looked natty. His trousers were always pressed. His hair was perfect. The cleft in his chiseled chin was still appealing, despite the evil I felt radiating from every one of his pores. But now he looked disheveled. His hair was matted to one side, and his clothes were streaked with something I could not identify—dirt? mud? feces? It was hard to tell. His face—normally a calm, cool facade—was a mask of desperation and frustration. One eye was nearly swollen closed, and his lip was split and bloodied.

"Yours?" I asked. I knew he was referring to the fentanyl. "If it *was* yours, you'd just take the loss. I think it belongs to someone else, someone who is going to hurt you if you don't get it back—and hurt you bad."

"*Going* to?" he raged. "*Going* to hurt me? Look at me! You think I haven't been hurt already?" It was clear that he had. He held the hammer parallel to his ear, not ready to strike, but ready to be ready.

"What happened?" I asked.

His eyes narrowed. "Drawing me into a sob story isn't going to work," he said.

I wasn't conscious of having said it as an empathy-building tactic. I was genuinely curious. But I could see why he would think so. The thing about dishonest people is that they can't conceive of anyone else actually being honest.

I changed the subject. "How did a guy like you get into

something like this? You're doing so well as a handler. You're well respected. What happened?"

I saw the hammer lower slightly. For a brief moment he looked down. "I...I needed a new rig."

In the dog show world, a "rig" usually refers to a bus-sized recreational vehicle, a home on wheels, specially kitted out with stacked dog crates. Handlers usually use them to travel from show to show with their dogs. But they can be outrageously expensive, costing more than a house in most parts of the country.

"But you have property in Gold Valley, one of the most expensive rural real estate markets in California. You have property in Mexico—"

"And I'm mortgaged to the hilt," he said, almost spitting with rage, as if not being able to have everything he coveted was a form of oppression.

I fumbled in the drawer behind me. My fingers closed on a boning knife. It was a thin blade, but it would have to do.

"Did you ever think that you could have avoided this whole situation by simply living within your means? I mean, did other people need to suffer because you're a greedy bastard?" I asked, although I knew the answer to that last question.

He answered my question with one of his own. "Are you forgetting who's holding the hammer?"

So that was a threat. "Jack is going to be here any moment," I lied.

"Your priest boyfriend couldn't hit the side of a barn with a tomcat," Teal seethed.

I feared he was right about that. Jack seemed pretty hopeless in the athletic department. I'm sure he could read anyone under the table, but that was hardly a threat. "Guess you're just going to have to deal with me," I said.

"I don't want to hurt you," he said. His shoulders sagged,

and I sensed there was truth in his words. I squeezed the handle of the boning knife, testing how it fit into my hand. "I just want the package back, so I can…"

"So you can pay your debt," I said.

"Yes," he said. I'd say he almost looked defeated, if he wasn't also oozing menace. A part of me felt sorry for him. It was a very, very small part.

"I'm sorry to tell you this, but I don't have it," I said.

"You're lying. You stole that dog—" His face turned red.

"Bree *recovered* a dog that belonged to her," I corrected him. "And yes, we found the fentanyl."

That stopped him. "But…how did you know what it was?"

"Because I gave it to the county sheriff, who sent it to the FBI lab. I imagine it's now safely in an evidence bag at the Sacramento field office. You should go ask *them* for it."

"Oh, Jesus," he said. He turned this way and that, as if looking for a way out. I could tell he was panicking and didn't know what to do about it. This thing had just gotten 110% more complicated and he was already not dealing well. "They're after me!" I wasn't sure exactly who "they" were, but I assumed he meant the FBI—in addition to the cartel goons. He looked back at me and sneered. "But you know that…"

A blood vessel in his forehead had grown to alarming proportions. He opened his mouth, and I expected a harangue, but instead he roared—he actually *roared*—his rage rendering him completely inarticulate. And it was at that moment that I realized my mistake. Before confessing to him that I didn't have it, he had had a reason to keep his wrath in check. But now—I had just handed him my shield.

He advanced on me, and his eyes swam with a rheumy mix of anger, frustration, and revenge.

I felt my breath quicken and my pulse began to race in my ears. He raised the hammer up, ready to strike. He took one step, two. His third would have had him on top of me, but I saw a blur in my peripheral vision.

Whipping my head around, I saw Scout in mid-flight. Boxers can jump as high as a person's chest—and she did. Something tells me Teal wasn't a tennis player, because he swung the hammer at her, but hit only the empty air. A split second later, Scout's front paws connected with his chest, punching him so hard that he toppled over backwards.

They don't call them Boxers for nothing.

He continued to swing the hammer, but he only succeeded in grazing her left flank. She was going for his throat, which she might have ripped out had he not protected it with his left elbow. She did draw blood, however, and I was not sorry to see it.

I leaped up and grabbed the hammer out of his hand. I jumped up, turned, and tossed the hammer into the sink. But his dominant hand, now free, went on the offense against Scout. He punched her in the head so hard that she yelped and rolled. I expected her to scramble to her feet, but instead she lay still, twitching.

A roar of my own burst from my throat, and I leaped on top of Teal. I pulled my right hand back, ready to strike with the boning knife. But he saw it and rolled. Unbalanced with the knife in the air, I toppled off of him. I scrambled to all fours, knife still in hand. I had lost my grip on the handle, however, and I felt the sting of the blade dig into the proximal phalanges of my fingers. Slick with my own blood now, I struggled to renew my grip on the handle.

This all happened in a split second. But Teal wasn't waiting around. He rose to his feet and wavered, as if he might topple again, dog or no dog. I crouched back on my haunches and sprang at him, pushing off against the bottom of the cabinets with my tennis shoes, leading with a head-butt and ready to strike with the knife as soon as I'd made contact.

But he was too quick for me. With a backhand I didn't see coming, he caught me in the jaw and spun me around. The knife flew out of my bloody hand, and I saw the counter coming toward me—fast and hard. I felt it connect with my skull, but at the same time it was as if I was watching it happen from another room. I felt pain, but I also felt strangely dissociated from it. My vision went black—I don't know how long, but it couldn't have been more than a second or two. When my vision rebooted, everything was fuzzy at first. Teal lumbered over me looking like the trunk of a blurry tree. I blinked and squinted, trying to bring my vision back into focus.

I heard a click, and my eyes resolved on a silver handgun pointed at my head. Then the vision in my right eye went out. Reaching up instinctively, I realized I wasn't blind—my eye was just full of blood, flowing from the new cut in my scalp.

Then I vomited. In the past, I always felt the vomiting coming on. Not this time. It just erupted from my throat, and I recognized it as a head injury symptom. *Great*, the voice in my head said as I felt the effluvia spatter over my face and neck.

"You made me do this," he said. "You didn't leave me any choice. I didn't want to hurt you."

His speaking of me in the past tense was both irritating and threatening. "I'm not ready to roll over and show you my belly," I said.

He pulled back the hammer on the pistol, and I glanced at his eyes. To my surprise, there was no anger there. Only desperation. "Teal, I can help you. Let me help you."

"There's nothing you can do," he said, the gun lowering a bit. Now it was only pointed at my chest.

"There is. I know these agents. I can talk to them—"

"Do you think I'm an idiot?"

I did, but that was beside the point. "I know things look bad, but killing me isn't going to make it better. It's only going to make it worse."

"How...how can it get worse?" he asked, and for a moment, I thought he might actually cry. But he got a grip on himself.

Out of the corner of my eye I saw Scout sit up. She whined quietly, looked around, and then scrambled to her feet, her claws finding limited purchase on the stone floor

Teal seemed either not to notice her or not to care. "Listen," I said, wanting to keep his attention on me, "let me brainstorm with you. I know people. I can help."

"You...are not going to help...me."

"Try me," I dared him. For a brief moment, he looked like he was actually considering it. But then his face hardened with resolve. Without speaking, he raised the pistol, aiming it level with my head. The voice in my head cried out, *No!* But not for myself. I knew that if he killed me, Scout would be next. But I felt a flicker of hope that he would see her utility as a mule for his fentanyl and let her live. She was a good-looking dog, and the customs agents at the border wouldn't know that she was beyond her showing years.

But even while my mind raced, agonizing over her fate, Scout took matters into her own paws. Springing up from behind Teal, she snatched at his hand—the hand holding the gun—and even before she hit the floor again began to shake it like a rodent's neck.

Teal howled again, but this time it was from the pain of being mauled by a Boxer with 230 pounds-per-square-inch of tensile strength in her jaws. Teal tried to shake her off his hand, but she held fast, growling nearly as loud as Teal was. The pistol exploded, but the bullet went wide—at least, if it did hit me, I didn't feel it.

I seized the moment and fell back to the floor, casting

around for the boning knife. My hand found it under the lip of the cabinet, and bloody and slick as my hands still were, I got a firm grip on the handle.

Teal swatted at Scout with his left hand, and then I saw him glance at the hammer in the sink. He struggled toward it, but before he could reach for it, I sprang on him again, raising the boning knife over my head, and driving it into the base of his neck, in a straight line toward his heart.

It was all automatic, of course. Some part of my brain must have been calculating, unconsciously knowing where the major arteries were and avoiding them. I wanted it to hurt, though. He yelped in agony and fell to one knee. Leaning over him, I balled my right hand into a fist and punched the handle of the boning knife, sending its point deeper into the cavity of his chest.

That did it. He fell limp, the gun falling from his hand to the floor with a loud clatter. Scout finally let go of his hand. "Good girl," I told her. Her eyes were wild, and her muzzle was wet and crimson with Teal's blood.

Teal slumped to the floor, no doubt passed out from the shock, from the pain. I checked his pulse. It was crazy fast and strong. I was betting one lung had collapsed. That was all right —he had another one. And I knew human anatomy well enough to be sure I hadn't done anything lethal.

Scout began sniffing around the body. Any moment now, she would engage in some primordial, instinctive canine victory ritual and start to roll in the pooling blood.

"Scout, no," I said. She hung her head and left him alone, coming back to me.

And that's when I lost it. I snatched at Scout's fur and smashed my face into her brindle side. I clutched at her and sobbed. My mouth was pressed against her skin, so the only sound that escaped was a muffled moan. She whined and sniffed at my ear.

Then my eyes sprang open. "Massaman," I said out loud. I pulled my phone from my pocket and dialed Special Agent Knight. I hit the speakerphone button and put the phone on the floor next to me.

"Dr. Gibbons?" Knight's voice, when it came, rose in question, in curiosity. I could hear the road noise just beneath her voice. They were still *en route*.

"Tammy, the man you captured, is he...a big man?"

"I'm a little sensitive about weight, Casey, but...yes, I'd call him a big man."

"Is he Asian?" I asked.

"Uh...he looks Hawaiian, or Samoan, or something," Knight admitted. "Why?"

"Because you nabbed the wrong man," I said.

"Darlin', have you been dippin' into the whiskey?"

"You don't have Teal—"

"And just how do you know that?" Knight asked.

"Because he's lying on the floor of my kitchen right now, in danger of bleeding out. And because he's a white, Anglo-Saxon asshole, not an Asian."

"Then who do we have in custody, sugar?"

What should I say? I wondered. He's a mobster? A hired thug? A criminal? "Uh..." I looked around the kitchen, grasping for a way to answer that didn't incriminate my...business associate.

My friend. I stopped short. Then I cleared my voice.

"He's my friend," I said. "He-he was worried about me, after he heard about the cottage. He was driving by to check up on me."

"Well, then, honey-pie, why didn't he just tell us that?"

"What did he say?" I asked.

"He hain't said a mumbling word," she answered.

"Good for him," I said.

"What? Just what do you mean by that?"

"Two white law enforcement agents arrest an innocent person of color. History is clear that anything he says or does is going to be twisted and used against him. He's a smart man. Of course he's kept his mouth shut."

"Well, it's prudent to check him out," Knight said.

"No, it isn't," I said, my voice rising. The last thing Massaman needed was to have his prints run. He got into this mess trying to protect me. I wasn't going to let him swing for it. "You arrested an innocent man. You have no cause to hold him. You need to turn around right now, bring my friend back to his car, and collect the *actual criminal*."

There was a long silence, but I heard the click of a turn signal and felt my shoulders relax. *Thank God,* I breathed inwardly.

"Casey, why is Teal bleeding out on your kitchen floor?"

"Because you were supposed to stop him and you didn't." I didn't intend to say that; it just came out, and near the end of it, my voice started to quiver. *Don't cry, dammit,* I commanded myself. *Don't you do it.*

"We'll be there just as fast as we can. We're headin' back now."

"Thank you," I said. I suddenly felt a little faint. "Can you call the local dispatch?" I asked. "We need an ambulance and probably a crime scene unit."

"On the way, darlin'. You just sit tight."

"Screw that," I said. "I need a whisky."

"Have two," Agent Knight said.

I hung up and hugged my dog again. Then Teal moaned. I jerked back, realizing I needed to restrain him somehow. Then Scout started barking. I shushed her, holding her snout closed—gently—with one hand. And then I heard what she heard.

A car was pulling up onto the gravel drive. It stopped. It was far too soon to be Agent Knight—they'd have to have been at the end of the block, and I knew they were at least halfway to Sacramento. Could it be Jack? But why? He'd know to steer clear for the FBI sting. Same with Gus. And I knew where Massaman was.

There was only one thing to do. I pressed Scout's head between my hands and looked into her eyes. I didn't want her to be distracted or to in any way misunderstand my next command: "Play dead, Scout." I scowled, and when I knew I had her attention, I said again, "Play dead. And keep your eyes shut this time."

I let her go and repeated the command. To my great relief, she dropped to the ground and turned nipples-up, feet in the air. I crawled a few feet away from Teal, slid the pistol across the floor in his direction, and fell on my face.

Then, I followed my own command. I concentrated on my breath, breathing so slowly that it would be undetectable—or so I hoped.

I heard a crash from the direction of the front door. Then I heard boots enter the kitchen. If the intruders were friendly, I knew they would have called my name and rushed to me. But that didn't happen.

Instead, the intruders laughed. They spoke English, but they didn't say much.

"He dead?" asked one. He had a deep voice that was so raspy he sounded like he'd been smoking since kindergarten.

A moment later, another, higher voice said, "No. Lotta blood, though."

The first man grunted. "He had to make it tough." He sighed. "Okay, load 'im up."

"What about her?" the second man asked.

"What are we, an ambulance? Leave her. Besides, she's probably dead. That's a lot of blood."

I sensed the second man kneeling near me. I concentrated on not wincing, expecting him to feel for a pulse. Instead, though, he straightened up. "Probably," he agreed. "Pretty dog."

"It *was* a pretty dog. Now it's just meat," the first man said.

"Okay, let's get him in to see the boss before he croaks on us," the second man said.

"My thoughts exactly."

I listened as they groaned and heaved. Then I heard their boots shuffle into the distance. A few moments later, I couldn't hear them at all. Getting to all fours, I saw Scout open one eye, and then roll onto her side. I touched her nose with the flat of my hand and reinforced the command verbally. "Stay."

Without thinking, I ducked out the back door and crept around the side of the cottage. I eased my head past the corner of the house, exposing just enough of myself to see what was happening with one eye.

Apparently, the men had loaded Teal into the back of a van, because I arrived just in time to see one of them close the rear door. The van was white—or at least a very light color, it was hard to tell in the yellow glow of the porch light. But I could see the license plate. "M335HT," I whispered over and over, forcing myself to remember the pattern. I withdrew from sight and hugged the wall, waiting for the van to drive away.

And as it did, I felt like my bones were turning to water. I let out a sigh so deep I thought my lungs would fold in on themselves. I didn't even realize I had been holding my breath. I ran to the back door and threw my arms around my dog again. I ran my hands over her frame, checking for injuries. I snatched a flashlight from the junk drawer and checked her pupils. They responded normally. She patiently endured all of this, and when I was finished with my inspection, I felt a sob of relief escape my throat. "That was good, Scout. Good girl. You are a *very* good girl."

I pulled out my phone again. My first call was to Agent Knight. I told her what had happened. I gave her the license plate number and the best description of the van that I could manage. Then I had that whiskey.

thirty-six

I woke up to a glaring sun in a sterile and unfamiliar place. It took me a minute to realize I was in a hospital room. Then it all came rushing back. I looked at my arms—an IV line emerged from a bandage on the back of my right hand. I didn't remember taking off my clothes. I did remember being taken to the hospital, but not much else.

"Scout!" I said aloud.

Just then, Jack walked in the door, holding a styrofoam cup that I took to be coffee. "Hey, sunshine," he said. He set the cup on the table next to the bed. "I'm guessing you need this more than I do right now."

"Where's Scout?" I asked.

"Shhhh...everything is fine. Gus called me last night after you left in the ambulance. I picked her up and brought her home. She's hanging out with Tripod and Abelard. She's just fine. Somehow, I seem to be collecting dogs at an alarming rate. I blame you." He scooted a chair closer to me and sat in it. "After I dropped her off, I came straight here."

"You've been here all night?" I asked.

"Remember who you're talking to. It happens more than you think."

I hadn't ever thought of it, but that made sense. I'm sure Jack sat in the hospital with more than one parishioner for a lengthy stretch, especially if they were dying.

He reached for my hand—the one without the needle, the one nearest him—and squeezed it. I squeezed back.

"You're really good to me," I said. "A girl could get used to this."

"I hope not. I feed on gratitude."

Despite the heaviness I felt, a laugh escaped me. "Are they going to come after me next?"

"Who, my love?" he asked.

Did he just call me "my love"? I felt a tangle of emotions. I decided to like it. I heaved a large sigh, and my shoulders relaxed a bit. "The...cartel goons."

"Well, Gus put a detail on your room. There are two deputies right outside the door."

"There are?"

"There are. He has a crush on you, you know. He's not going to let anything happen to you."

"I know he does."

"I will confess to feeling a little jealous," he said, smiling. "But I can't begrudge him too much. I got the girl."

I didn't like being talked about as if I was a ring-toss prize at the county fair, but I let it slide. You have to pick your battles. And I was just too exhausted—and indebted—for this one.

"But I have to watch my ass," he continued. "If I'm ever down for the count, he's going to swoop in."

That did it. I narrowed my eyes. "You talk as if I am devoid of agency."

He laughed. Hard. It was a big belly laugh. I didn't get it. "What?"

"Oh, no one doubts you have agency. You and Scout are alive because you have freaking buttloads of agency."

"And don't forget it," I said.

"That would require dementia, I think." He brought my hand to his mouth and kissed it. I felt a stream of warmth travel down my spine and pool in my belly.

Just then I heard a knock. I looked up and saw Ajeet waiting by the door. He looked cowed and uncomfortable. In one hand he held a bouquet of daisies. In the other a cloth shopping bag. "Is...this a good time?" he asked.

Jack rose and turned the chair toward him. "It is an excellent time. I was just on my way to get myself a cup of coffee." He turned back and winked at me. "See you in a few."

I nodded. Ajeet, looking about as uncomfortable as I have ever seen him, sat in the chair. He fumbled with the flowers in his lap.

"Can you put those here on my bed?" I asked, patting the spot beside me.

"Of course," he said, looking relieved. He placed the flowers gingerly on the thin tan blanket and gave me an awkward smile. "Are you all right?" he asked.

"I'm going to live, I think, unless outside forces intervene," I answered. "I needed stitches in my hand and my scalp." I pointed to the bandage on my head.

"Was it bad?" he asked.

"Grade three concussion," I said.

"Ouch. You lost consciousness?"

"Not at first, thank God. But there are lots of gaps in my memory from last night—I mean, it was last night, wasn't it? What day is it?"

"Wednesday," he said.

"Okay. Yes. Last night. I remember the ambulance showing up. After that, it's bits-and-pieces."

He nodded. He looked impossibly sad. "I was very angry at you," he said.

The fact that he used the past tense gave me a thrill of hope. "I know you were," I said. We sat for several long moments of uncomfortable silence. "Are you still planning to leave the clinic?" I asked.

He looked away from me, never a good sign. He sighed. "When I was in veterinary school, we had this cat come into our clinic. The cat was a little wobbly. I told the owners all of the possible diagnoses."

"And?"

"No, I don't think you understand," he said. "I told them *all* of the possible outcomes—from arthritis to rabies. My supervisor was furious at me. He interrupted me and took over the exam. He tried to save the situation, but I had so upset the clients that they took their cat elsewhere."

"Oh, dear," I said.

"That was the day I learned about oversharing." He smiled grimly. "But I had been *trying* to do everything right. I wanted them to make an informed decision. It did not occur to me that I had overwhelmed them and...scared them off."

"That sounds really painful. But you *did* learn," I said.

"I did learn," he agreed. His eyes flitted up, met mine, and held them. "Have you...learned?" he asked.

"I have," I said. And it was true. It had been wrong to use Ajeet's class to get Betty Swann's rivals out of their houses, and I regretted it.

He reached over and patted my hand. "Then let us say no more about it." He leaned over and pulled a thermos and a cup from his cloth grocery bag. "May I pour you a cup of chai?"

"Does it have more sugar than tea in it?" I asked.

He waggled his head. "It is not chai if it is not so sweet that it makes your teeth hurt."

"Well, then, I suppose I need to have the authentic experience. Set me up." I had another motive. What I really wanted was a whisky, but I was pretty sure the hospital would frown on that. Sugar was a poor substitute for alcohol, but hey, any port in a storm.

I watched as he poured a steaming cup of the light-brown liquid. He smiled—a gladder smile this time—and set the mug in front of me. I sniffed at it, and it smelled luxurious, exotic, divine. I took a sip. My eyes widened instantly. "That is... delicious."

"Have you never had chai before?" he asked, pouring himself a cup as well.

"I guess I haven't. I've never tasted anything like that."

"Well, then, welcome to my world." He held up his own cup and I clinked mine to it. I took another sip. He was right. My teeth ached, it was so sweet. It was wonderful.

He pulled something from his shirt pocket. It looked like a stick of lip balm. "This is a homeopathic preparation that will reduce inflammation and pain and stimulate white blood cell production. It will also balance your aura. Hold two of them under your tongue until they dissolve, every two hours."

I took it. I screwed the cap off and saw that the tube was filled with little white tablets about the size of a baby aspirin. My personal, scientific opinion was that homeopathy was a load of hooey, but I didn't want to be ungracious. "Uh...thanks, Ajeet. You didn't need to do that."

He waggled his head again. "I want you to be well. I also want you back to work. I don't relish taking up your slack."

I laughed at that and set the container of pills on the little table beside the bed. "I'm glad you're staying," I said.

"And I...I am glad you are going to be all right."

thirty-seven

My first day back at work was grueling. I didn't realize how depleted I was. I'd never had a head injury before; it was definitely unexplored territory. I decided I'd rather have a broken arm any day. I felt in danger of nodding off most of the time. I drank so much coffee my fingers were vibrating. I felt sick.

Even worse, however, was jumping out of my skin at the slightest noise. A part of my brain told me it was PTSD, but I usually ignore that part of my brain. It might tell me the truth, but it rarely tells me anything practical or useful in the moment.

I wasn't cleared to drive yet, so when the seemingly interminable day finally did come to an end, I walked out into the parking lot to find Jack waiting for me. He must have been on his way back from a visit with a parishioner, because he was dressed all in his natty blacks and was wearing his clerical collar.

I got in the car, and he leaned over and kissed me. I surrendered to the kiss and felt warmth flood into my belly. "You okay?" he asked.

"Yeah. Just tired."

"Let's get you home. I have dinner in the oven. And then you can go straight to bed."

"That sounds wonderful. But I want a bath."

"You got it."

Scout and I were still staying with Jack, mostly because the doctor didn't think I should be alone until they knew more about how my head injury was healing up. And that could take a long time. Jack had given me the spare room and had even cleared it out to make it more inviting. But I mostly used it just to house my suitcase. Most nights I crawled in bed with him.

We still hadn't made love. But just being held by him felt like salvation. I know how men are, testosterone being what it is, but Jack never tendered an advance. Aside from kisses and caresses and terms of endearment, he let me lead. In any other man, I'd call it superhuman. But Jack was not an ordinary man. And the idea of sinking into sleep snuggled up to him seemed like the perfect end to a very difficult day.

My phone buzzed. I sighed and reached for it. "What now?"

"Text?" Jack asked, turning left toward his church.

"Yeah."

"Probably just a Viagra ad," he predicted.

"It's from Sarge," I said, my eyebrows bunching as I read. "He wants us to come to the diner after closing. He says it's important."

"You're exhausted—" Jack began to protest.

He was right, but I cut him off. "Sarge wouldn't ask if it wasn't important."

Jack sighed. "When is the diner closed?"

"At eight."

"Tell you what," Jack said. "Let's go home and eat, and you get your bath. Then, if you feel like it, we'll go."

"You don't need to go," I said.

"Unless you specifically tell me not to go, I'm going," Jack said.

I nodded. "Okay. What's for dinner?"

———

Dinner turned out to be a pot roast with root vegetables, swimming in so much gravy it was almost a stew. It was also so tender it melted in my mouth. It was wonderful. So was my bath. I no sooner lowered myself into the steaming water than I felt all the tension drain out of me as if by magic. I lay in the tub and read the latest JAVMA—*Journal of the American Veterinary Medical Association*—on my tablet until the water grew cold. My limbs felt like spaghetti as I emerged.

Jack had already fed the dogs, and they were passed out on their dog beds near the fireplace, all three of them. Scout stirred when she saw me but didn't bother to actually get up.

At that point I would have preferred to go to bed, but the bath had restored me. Jack looked a bit deflated when I announced I still wanted to go to Millie's, but he didn't protest. "Okay. Let's get it over with so that you can come home and rest."

I gave him a kiss on the cheek and grabbed a sweater. I gave the dogs a pat, and we headed out. We didn't say much on the way over, but it wasn't because Jack was pouting or anything. I think we were both just tired puppies, and conversation was more effort than either of us had the bandwidth for. That was okay. One of the things I liked about Jack was his comfort with silence. It's not like he was a guy who didn't talk much—he loved to talk. But he seemed to cherish silence as well. The man has *range.*

We pulled up at Millie's Diner and waited at the front door for Sarge to come and unlock it. We caught his eye and he smiled as he walked across the dining room toward the door, followed by the wagging figure of Prince, his Cavalier King Charles Spaniel. He turned a key that must have already been resident in the lock. "I'm so glad ya'll could come," he said, opening the door. "Got someone waiting for you."

He waved us toward a round booth. I stopped to give Prince a pet, and then we slid into our seats. Aside from Sarge and his dog, the place appeared to be completely empty, and therefore, eerily quiet. Sarge moved quickly with an uncanny grace for a man his size. He set plates down in the middle of the table— bacon-wrapped dates and what turned out to be a spiced lentil dip with tortilla chips. He then brought over a bucket full of ice and bottled beer.

He hovered then and glanced toward the rest rooms. A door opened and I was shocked to see Massaman emerge, cradling Jok, his pink hairless cat.

"Massaman, I'm so glad you're all right," I blurted out.

"I could say the same," he said. He sat in the booth next to Jack and Sarge squeezed in next to me. Sarge distributed the beer. "I'm sorry I wasn't able to intervene when Teal attacked you," Massaman said. "I was...detained."

"Yes, I know. And I'm so sorry about that."

"It wasn't your fault," he said, tossing a dismissal with his voluminous chin. "And besides, it was thanks to your efforts that I was released without...further scrutiny. I am in your debt."

I wasn't sure what to say to that. It was certainly a reversal of position, given Massaman's typical relationship with me—

and, I assume, others. This was a rare sort of privilege I would never have even entertained.

Sarge cleared his throat. "I called ya'll together here because we got a problem. We got a cartel that still holds Casey responsible—in part—for their loss. And I don't expect them to just drop it."

"What happened to Teal?" I asked.

"Teal is...no longer a matter of concern," Massaman said, pulling his lips back in an ominous smile.

"What? Did you kill him?" I asked.

"No, no, no. But don't forget, I have been in this cartel's employ. I...hear things."

I nodded. "I'm grateful that you all are concerned about me," I said. "But right now, I'm more worried about Teal's assistant and the dogs he still has. Is the cartel just going to carry on?"

Sarge looked at his beefy hands and nodded. "It's a profitable business model. I don't see why they wouldn't."

"The assistant—Oscar Schwartz," Jack said. "Do you know if he really *wants* to carry on?"

Massaman shook his head. "My...sources tell me that he is in over his head. If he could, he'd flee far and fast. Which is just where his employers want him."

"If he's scared, then they own him," I said.

"Yes," Massaman agreed.

"He's in bondage," Jack said.

I nudged Jack in the side. "Do you have to think of everything in biblical terms?"

"Yes," he answered.

I gave him a look. Then I said, "So how do we get the cartel to release Oscar from his bondage, along with the dogs?"

"And leave you alone, while they're at it?" Sarge added.

Massaman shook his head and stroked the top of the head

of the cat in his lap. "You don't." Jok's eyes were half-closed, clearly blissed out by this attention.

Jack set down his beer bottle and spread his hands on the table, fingers wide. "The early Christians were in the habit of ransoming captives—not just other Christians, but especially the poor, no matter what their religion—people who couldn't buy their own freedom. It was a corporal act of mercy."

A slight smile broke out on Massaman's lips, and his eyes narrowed until they were almost as lidded as Jok's.

"What you gettin' at, preacher?" Sarge asked.

"What about a payout?" Jack let that sink in for a moment, and then continued. "I'm thinking...maybe we could make it worth the cartel's while to walk away from this operation, including Casey. We give them the cash, and they leave Casey alone—forever. They also leave Mr. Schwartz alone. And the dogs. They'll have enough to buy off a new trainer, if they want to keep up this...business model. But they'd have to agree to move on."

Massaman reached for a chip and dipped it in the lentils. "Buttered curry," he said approvingly.

"It's actually Dal Makhani," Sarge said.

Massaman grunted his approval.

"Absolutely not," I said. "For one thing, where would we get that kind of money?"

"What kind of money would we be talking about?" Jack asked.

Massaman shrugged. "The lost 'package' was worth about $15,000," he said with his mouth full. "We could float $25,000."

Sarge groaned. "Teal lost his life for a measly $15,000? That's crazy."

"If you don't have it, you don't have it," I said.

"He coulda sold his motor home," Sarge argued.

"And then how would he make his living?" I asked. "No, he was definitely between a rock and a hard place."

"Let's do it," Jack said.

"I am not paying drug dealers $25,000," I protested. I reached hesitantly for a bacon-wrapped date. I'd heard of such things but hadn't actually tried one.

"No, I will," Jack said.

"Where the hell are you going to get $25,000?" I asked.

"I'm not in the priesthood for money," Jack said. "My family is wealthy."

"They *are* Episcopalians," Sarge said.

"There are poor Episcopalians," Jack narrowed one eye.

"That's an oxymoron if I ever heard one," Sarge said.

"I am not going to let you cough up $25,000 on my account," I said, with impressive finality.

"Stop me," Jack said, seeing my finality and raising it.

"I don't think it will work," Massaman said, shaking his head. "The enterprise is too profitable."

"Offer them $30,000 then," Jack said.

"Jack!" I yelled.

He held his hand up to ward off my protest.

"You cannot save everyone, Father," Massaman said.

"You're wrong about that," Jack said. "*Everyone* will be saved. Everything broken will be healed. Everyone lost will be found. It will just take time."

Massaman chuckled. "I do not share your metaphysical optimism, but I admire it."

"I think Jack is onto something," Sarge said. "Think about it, now. It isn't just about this being a profitable scheme for the cartel. There are other factors in play. The FBI is onto them. The cartel is going to want to lay low for a while. It would be in their interest to accept Jack's deal. There's at least a profit in the short term. Cutting Oscar and the dogs loose might be safer for them than trying to keep the operation intact but dormant."

Massaman stroked his chin. "I had not thought of that."

"No," I said. "I'm not going to let you pay $30,000 of your family's money to buy off a bunch of criminals."

"I don't think you have the power to stop me," Jack said.

"Is that the way it's going to be?" I asked.

"To keep you safe?" Jack asked. "I'd pay a thousand times that. And risk estrangement. Just so long as I knew you were alive and well."

It's impossible to stay mad at a man like that. I didn't try. I sighed my defeat. I was still holding the bacon-wrapped date.

"Are you going to eat that?" Sarge asked, "Or just wave it around?"

I put it into my mouth and my eyes widened as the complex, amazing flavors took over my mouth and made it their own. "O my god, that's amazing," I said.

"Thank you," Sarge said.

"I will make the offer," Massaman said. "If they agree, how soon can you have the money?"

"I can wire it within an hour," Jack said.

Massaman nodded. "I'll let you know."

epilogue

The next day I was on pins and needles at work—again. I had just finished with a client a bit earlier than I thought, which actually gave me time to hit the restroom. Or it would have if it hadn't been occupied. I leaned against the counter by the microscope and picked at my nails. Then Ellie came out of the restroom.

"Any word?" she asked. I shook my head. She pressed her lips together in concern and squeezed my elbow. Then she returned to her desk. I made use of the restroom and just as I was drying my hands my phone buzzed. I snatched at it, grabbing it out of my lab coat pocket. But my hands were still wet and I dropped it on the floor.

"Egads," I said. Bending down to pick it up, I hit my head on the sink. Hard. I clutched at my head with my right hand and finally succeeded in retrieving my phone with the other. I left the bathroom, only to encounter Stacy waiting outside the door.

"What was that noise?" she asked.

"I tried to break the sink with my head bone," I said.

Her face screwed up into a judgmental scowl. "On purpose?"

"No, of course not on purpose," I snapped. I sighed with more exasperation than I wanted to show. "I'm sorry. I'm just... stressed."

"Anything you want to tell me about?" Stacy asked.

Absolutely not, the voice in my head yelled. "No...but thank you," I said.

Stacy went into the restroom, and I finally got a look at my phone. Hoping against hope it would be from Massaman, or Sarge, or even Jack, my shoulders slumped when I saw that it was from Fuchsia Carhart.

"Movement on the lawsuit. Meet up for a drink?"

So Fuchsia was mixing business and pleasure. *Well, why not?* I thought. *A spoonful of sugar and all that.*

I texted back, suggesting a time. Then I grabbed the next file from the hopper and cleaned maggots out of a dog's ear. Oh, the glamour.

Just before lunch my phone buzzed again. I grabbed it out of my pocket, being careful not to drop it this time, even though there were no predatory sinks in sight. It was Jack, and it was a phone call, not a text.

I raced for the break room and closed the door. Ellie was in there, her eyebrows rising as I ran in and closed the door behind me.

"Hi," I said after pushing the green button on my phone.

"Hey there," Jack said.

"Any news?" I asked.

"Yes. They took the deal. I just wired the money. It's done. You're safe. And so are the dogs. Oscar Schwartz is safe, too, thanks be to God."

"That's...that's great. I'll ask Ellie to call the dogs' owners this afternoon. When can we pick them up?" I made eye contact with Ellie, who gave me a thumbs-up.

"Massaman is going to have a conversation with Oscar this afternoon. Depending on how that goes, he might drop some of the dogs off there at the clinic."

"We can handle that," I said, remembering that our kennels were currently empty. "Jack, I still feel terrible about you spending your money this way."

I could almost hear him shrug over the phone. "Eh. It's just money. It's not like it's important."

"Spoken like a true man of privilege," I said.

"Guilty as charged, I'm afraid," he said. "Which is why I don't mind putting it to good use."

"What use was it put to before you spent it on us?"

"It was invested in micro-loans supporting women-owned businesses in developing countries."

"Oh." That shut me up. "Now I feel bad that we're taking money away from poor women."

"You can't do it all," Jack said.

"No," I agreed. My emotions were a tangle of gratitude, shame, and regret. I didn't know how to sort them out.

"Dinner tonight?" Jack asked.

"Uh...I'm meeting Fuchsia for drinks after work. There's been a development in the lawsuit."

"Ah. Well then, a late dinner at my house?"

"I have a better idea," I said. "How about you bring the dogs to the cottage at eight, along with some takeout?"

"That sounds like a great idea," he agreed.

"Good. See you then."

"You're gathering no moss," Ellie said as I put the phone in my lab coat pocket. "And you're blushing."

I turned quickly away from her and opened the door. I

knew full well that when I got home from my meeting with Fuchsia, I'd be feeling a little loose. And no doubt Jack would bring a single malt to celebrate. I wondered if he'd end up staying the night and realized that I wanted him to. It was the kind of night a priest could get lucky.

•·